EDGE

EDGE

COLLECTED STORIES

M. E. KERR

OPEN ROAD

INTEGRATED MEDIA

NEW YORK

"Do You Want My Opinion?" *Seventeen* magazine, 1985
and in Don Gallo's *Sixteen*, 1984.

"The Perfume of Goodbye." *Visions*, edited by Don Gallo, Delacourt Press, 1988.

"Sunny Days and Sunny Nights." *Cicada*, March/April, 1999.

"Son of a One Eye." Scholastic *Scope*, 1989.

"The Author." *Funny You Should Ask*, edited by David Gale, Delacourt Press, 1992.

"We Might As Well All Be Strangers." *Am I Blue*,
edited by Marion Dane Bauer, HarperCollins, 1995.

"Like Father, Like Son." Scholastic *Scope*, 1995.

"I Will Not Think of Maine." *Family Secrets*, edited by Lisa Rowe Fraustino,
Viking, 1998.

"I've Got Gloria." Delacourt Press, 1997.

"Grace." *I Believe in Water*, HarperCollins, 2000.

"Guess Who's Back in Town, Dear?" *Stay True*, Scholastic Press, 1998.

"The Green Killer." *Bad Behavior*, edited by Mary Higgins Clark,
Harcourt Brace& Company, 1998.

"Great Expectations." *On the Fringe*, Penguin Group, 1991.

"I'll See You When This War Is Over." *Shattered*, Knopf, 2003.

"The Fire at Far and Away." St. Martins Press, 2004.

Copyright © 2015 by M. E. Kerr

Cover design by Connie Gabbert

978-1-5040-0991-1

Published in 2015 by Open Road Integrated Media, Inc.
345 Hudson Street
New York, NY 10014
www.openroadmedia.com

CONTENTS

DO YOU WANT MY OPINION?

The night before last I dreamed that Cynthia Slater asked my opinion of *The Catcher in the Rye*.

Last night I dreamed I told Lauren Lake what I thought about John Lennon's music, Picasso's art, and Soviet-American relations.

It's getting worse.

I'm tired of putting my head under the cold-water faucet.

Early this morning my father came into my room and said, "John, are you getting serious with Eleanor Rossi?"

"Just because I took her out three times?"

"Just because you sit up until all hours of the night talking with her!" he said. "We know all about it, John. Her mother called your mother."

I didn't say anything. I finished getting on my socks and shoes.

He was standing over me, ready to deliver the lecture.

It always started the same way.

"You're going to get in trouble if you're intimate, John. You're too young to let a girl get a hold on you."

"Nobody has a hold on me, Dad."

1

"Not yet. But one thought leads to another. Before you know it, you'll be exploring all sorts of ideas together, knowing each other so well you'll finish each other's sentences."

"Okay," I said. "Okay."

"Stick to lovemaking."

"Right," I said.

"Don't discuss ideas."

"Dad," I said, "kids today—"

"Not nice kids. Aren't you a nice kid?"

"Yeah, I'm a nice kid."

"And Eleanor, too?"

"Yeah, Eleanor, too."

"Then show some respect for her. Don't ask her opinions. I know it's you who starts it."

"Okay," I said.

"Okay?" he said. He mussed up my hair, gave me a poke in the ribs, and went down to breakfast.

By the time I got downstairs, he'd finished his eggs and was sipping coffee, holding hands with my mother.

I don't think they've exchanged an idea in years.

To tell you the truth, I can't imagine them exchanging ideas, ever, though I know they did. She has a collection of letters he wrote to her on every subject from Shakespeare to Bach, and he treasures this little essay she wrote for him when they were engaged, on her feelings about French drama.

All I've ever seen them do is hug and kiss. Maybe they wait until I'm asleep to get into their discussions. Who knows?

I walked to school with Edna O'Leary.

She's very beautiful. I'll say that for her. We put our arms around each other, held tight, and stopped to kiss along the way. But I'd never ask her opinion on any subject. She just doesn't appeal to me that way.

"I love your eyes, John," she said.

"I love your smile, Edna."

"Do you like this color on me?"

"I like you in blue better."

"Oh, John, that's interesting, because I like you in blue, too."

We chatted and kissed and laughed as we went up the winding walk to school.

In the schoolyard everyone was cuddled up except for some of the lovers, who were off walking in pairs, talking. I doubted that they were saying trivial things. Their fingers were pointing and their hands were moving, and they were frowning.

You can always tell the ones in love by their passionate gestures as they get into conversations.

I went into the Boys' room for a smoke.

That's right, I'm starting to smoke. That's the state of mind I'm in.

My father says I'm going through a typical teenage stage, but I don't think he understands how crazy it's making me. He says he went through the same thing, but I just can't picture that.

On the bathroom wall there were heads drawn with kids' initials inside.

There was the usual graffiti:

Josephine Merril is a brain. I'd like to know her opinions!

If you'd like some interesting conversation, try Loulou.

I smoked a cigarette and thought of Lauren Lake.

Who didn't think of Lauren? I made a bet with myself that

there were half a dozen guys like me remembering Lauren's answer to Mr. Porter's question last week in Thoughts class.

A few more answers like that, and those parents who want Thoughts taken out of the school curriculum will have their way. Some kid will run home and tell the folks what goes on in Porter's room, and Thoughts will be replaced by another course in history, language, body maintenance, sex education, or some other boring subject that isn't supposed to be provocative.

"What are dreams?" Mr. Porter asked.

Naturally, Lauren's hand shot up first She can't help herself. "Lauren?"

"Dreams can be waking thoughts or sleeping thoughts," she said. "I had a dream once, a waking one, about a world where you could say anything on your mind, but you had to be very careful about who you touched. You could ask anyone his opinion, but you couldn't just go up and kiss him."

Some of the kids got red-faced and sucked in their breaths. Even Porter said, "Now, take it easy, Lauren. Some of your classmates aren't as advanced as you are."

One kid yelled out, "If you had to be careful about touching, how would you reproduce in that world?"

"The same way we do in our world," Lauren said, "only lovemaking would be a special thing. It would be the intimate thing, and discussing ideas would be a natural thing."

"That's a good way to cheapen the exchange of ideas!" someone muttered.

Everyone was laughing and nudging the ones next to them, but my mind was spinning. I bet other kids were about to go out of their minds, too.

4

Mr. Porter ran back and kissed Lauren.

She couldn't seem to stop.

She said, "What's wrong with a free exchange of ideas?"

"Ideas are personal," someone said. "Bodies are all alike, but ideas, are individual and personal."

Mr. Porter held Lauren's hand. "Keep it to yourself, Lauren," he said. "Just keep it to yourself."

"In my opinion," Lauren began, but Mr. Porter had to get her under control, so he just pressed his mouth against hers until she was quiet.

"Don't tell *everything* you're thinking, darling," he warned her. "I know this is a class on thoughts, but we have to have *some* modesty."

Lauren just can't quit. She's a brain, and that mind of hers is going to wander all over the place. It just is. She's that kind of girl.

Sometimes I think I'm that kind of boy, and not the nice boy I claim to be. Do you know what I mean? I want to tell someone what I think about the books I read, not just recite the plots. And I want to ask someone what she thinks about World War II, not just go over its history. And I want to . . .

Nevermind.

Listen—the heck with it!

It's not what's up there that counts.

Love makes the world go round. Lovemaking is what's important—relaxing your body, letting your mind empty—just feeling without thinking—just giving in and letting go.

There'll be time enough to exchange ideas, make points—all of it. I'll meet the right girl someday and we'll have the rest of our lives to confide in each other.

"Class come to order!" Mr. Porter finally got Lauren quieted down. "Now, a dream is a succession of images or ideas present in the mind mainly during sleep. It is an involuntary vision . . ."

On and on, while we all reached for each other's hands, gave each other kisses, and got back to normal.

I put that memory out of my poor messed-up mind, and put out my cigarette.

I was ready to face another day, and I told myself, Hey, you're going to be okay. Tonight, you'll get Dad's car, get a date with someone like Edna O'Leary, go off someplace and whisper loving things into her ear, and feel her soft long blond hair tickle your face, tell her you love her, tell her she's beautiful . . .

I swung through the door of the Boys' room, and headed down the hall, whistling, walking fast.

Then I saw Lauren, headed right toward me.

She looked carefully at me, and I looked carefully at her.

She frowned a little. I frowned a lot.

I did everything to keep, from blurting out, "Lauren, what do you think about outer space travel?" . . . "Lauren, what do you think of Kurt Vonnegut's writing?" . . . "Lauren, do you think the old Beatles' music is profound or shallow?"

For a moment my mind went blank while we stood without smiling or touching.

Then she kissed my lips, and I slid my arm around her waist.

"Hi, John, dear!" She grinned.

"Hi, Lauren, sweetheart!" I grinned back.

I almost said, "Would you like to go out tonight?" But it isn't fair to ask a girl out when all you really want is one thing.

I held her very close to me and gently told her that her hair smelled like the sun, and her lips tasted as sweet as red summer apples. Yet all the while I was thinking, Oh, Lauren, we're making a mistake with China, in my opinion. . . . Oh, Lauren, Lauren, from your point of view, how do things look in the Middle East?

THE SWEET PERFUME
OF GOOD-BYE

Here nothing smells.

Almost nothing smells.

The roses are red beyond belief but give off no aroma. The lemons are as yellow as the sun, but there is no lemony fragrance, just a semblance of bitterness as you bite into one. The fresh-cut bright green grass where my lovers sit does not even smell, as it did summer mornings when I was on Earth and could smell it from my room while the boy cut our lawn.

I call them "my lovers" with a little smile. That is my sense of humor emerging (though I am thought to be a humorless young scientist). They do not make love to me, of course. They are mine only in the fact that I am studying them.

Here the only perfume is the sweet perfume of good-bye that comes on a person one hour before death. I cannot describe it accurately, even though I am a stickler for accuracy. Like our lilies? A little, but more rare and tantalizing, and people rush to be near whoever is dying, keeping a respectful distance (scores of them behind me as I write this), but still lingering nearby for a faint whiff.

Carlo, the boy, is dying. He has just begun to give off this haunting, beautiful scent. His girlfriend, Marny, is ecstatic as she breathes it in. They sit on the grass near me, having their last conversation.

I can hear them. It is love talk of the passionate variety.

The great advantage of being thought to be crazy is that I can sit near them and they ignore me. Let her be, they say. The poor thing, they say. We have so much and she has nothing but her mixed-up brain, they say.

It is important for you to know that there is no murder here, no suicide, no wars, no illness. The only way you can die is naturally, when your time comes, and no one knows when that will be.

Carlo is my age, seventeen.

I have a certain freak value here.

They ask me to be on late-night television talk shows of the kooky variety.

They pretend to treat me with respect, but no matter who the host is, there is always the slanted smile, the wink I am not supposed to see, the same questions.

"So what is Earth like?"

"Filled with the most magnificent fragrances!" I respond.

"Is everyone there an hour away from death then?" Ha! Ha! from the studio audience, but I persist. "No, listen! Our flowers smell. Our food smells. The very air smells. Not always good. We have bad smells too."

"So you spend all your time on Earth mesmerized by these odors, ah? How do you get anything done on Earth? How did your people ever build that fantastic spaceship you supposedly came here in, if you have all these odors to distract you?"

"We take our scents for granted, you see."

"Of course! Of course! And does your spaceship smell?"

The audience is bent double with laughter, and it is just as well in this phase of the interview, for I am not to disclose anything about the mission, not even in jest, not even here in this report.

I am to concentrate on Farfire.

That is what they call this place.

I was chosen because of my practical nature, my keen ability to be objective and unemotional. I am my father's daughter. Doctor Orr remarks on it often, telling me that I am rational and unstirrable beyond my years.

"Tell me, Caroline—is that your Earth name or your Farfire name—Caroline?"

"It is my Earth name. I am not from Farfire, so I have no Farfire name."

"Caroline's not too unlike a Farfire name, though, is it?"

"There is a lot of similarity between Earth and Farfire."

"Yes, well, tell me, Caroline, do you have death on Earth too?"

"Of course we have death."

"Of course you have death." His tone mocks me again. "Except when you Earth folks die, there is no odor." Big wink to the studio audience.

"Not a good one, no."

"What's a bad odor, pray tell?" and there is more laughter.

"I can't describe it. Burnt rubber. Dead flowers. Feces. Those are bad odors on Earth."

"Feces smell on Earth?"

"Yes, they do," and the audience is in convulsions again.

"Well, Earth must not be all that lovely. You must be glad to be on Farfire, hah?"

I was, in the beginning. I truly was. Anticipating it, before I left, with pleasure. Challenged when I arrived. All of it new. But I did not calculate this part of it, being taken for a laughable freak, the way on Earth we treat those who say they've seen flying saucers or been to Mars.

"You'll not be there long," Father reassured me. "The moment you hear three beeps in your earpiece, use your minimike to assure Doctor Orr you're going directly to the field where you were dropped. He'll get you home safely in about two years, just in time for your nineteenth birthday!" Father was excited. "There's no telling what you'll learn about your Farfire teenage counterparts!"

"But will I blend in?" I asked him. "Will they take me captive? Will I be in any danger?"

"They will treat you as interlopers have been treated from time immemorial."

"How is that?"

"They will find some way to trivialize you. They will not believe you. It's all to your advantage."

"Caroline, Marny and I saw you on television," Carlo calls over to me. If anything could ruffle me, it would be that exquisite fragrance, almost making me homesick, it's so voluptuous. "We want to ask you a question." His lopsided smile reminds me of the talk show hosts. "How," says Carlo, "do you know someone's dying on your Earth, if there is no perfume?"

I try to tell him, but his eyes glaze over as I start to describe traffic accidents, war, heart disease, all of it, and Marny giggles into her hands.

"How," Carlo interrupts me as though he is bored with my

ranting and raving, "do you handle death then? Death sounds like something horrible."

"How," I come back with a testiness that surprises me, "do you handle the idea that in about forty-five minutes you won't ever be with Marny again?"

He laughs gaily. "We will have been together for as long as we were intended to be together. What more can anyone want?"

Marny asks, "On Earth, do people die at the same time?"

"No, but . . ." I have no ready answer. "But we don't like death."

"What sense does that make?" Carlo says. "Everyone must die. It can't go on forever."

In a while they prepare for his funeral.

They sing:

> *My! My! My! I smell good-bye!*
> *I know you've got to go*
> *So one last kiss*
> *The scent is bliss!*
> *Good-bye, the scent's to die!*

They all wear white and dance.

Marny can't stop smiling with joy.

There is nothing ever said about God here.

After the funeral I ask Marny if there is religion, God, what?

"All of that is after death," she says.

"But what exactly do you believe happens after death?"

"We don't know," she says, and her mouth tips in a grin. "I suppose on Earth you do?"

"We have certain beliefs," I say. "We have concepts. There is a concept of heaven, and a concept or hell. Now, heaven is . . ." and even as I talk, Marny wanders off from me, yawning, calling over her shoulder that she'd really like to hear all about it . . . some other time.

I have never been treated so rudely. That is the part that is so hard to bear: me, Caroline Aylesworth, winner of so many, many honors in science my bookshelves cannot hold all the gold statuettes, my walls with no room left for framed certificates. Not even *listened* to here on Farfire!

I cannot say that I am in any way disappointed when I hear the three beeps, even though this tiny taste of Farfire *has* provoked considerable curiosity in me . . . and even though there is no way ever again to have that curiosity satisfied, for there is no returning here.

"Hello, Caroline!" I hear Doctor Orr's familiar voice. "Do you think you got a good sample?"

"Not a comprehensive one, by any means, but enough about Farfire to make a highly interesting report."

"Excellent! And you know how to find your way to the field?"

"Of course I do."

"I'm here now, waiting for you."

"Give me about an hour and fifteen minutes."

"Gladly," Doctor Orr answers. "My God, Caroline, I'm almost overwhelmed by this wonderful fragrance here!"

"A fragrance, Doctor Orr? Not on Farfire. You see—"

He interrupts me with a whoop of joy. "*Un*believable! Almost

like lilies! It's come upon me suddenly! Caroline? It's so all per-
vasive! It's on *me!* My hands, my face—it's the sweetest perfume!"

Of course, I cannot get to him in time.

I sit down right where I am and make my entry.

I write, *I think I've lost my ride home.*

In the interest of accuracy, I cross out "I think."

SUNNY DAYS
AND SUNNY NIGHTS

Females prefer chunky peanut butter over smooth, forty-three percent to thirty-nine percent," Alan announces at dinner, "while men show an equal liking for both."

My father likes this conversation. I think even my mother does, since she is telling Alan enthusiastically that she likes smooth. Moments before, she confided that she preferred red wine, after Alan said that women are more likely than men to order wine in a restaurant, and a majority prefer white.

Alan is filled with this sort of information.

He wants to become an advertising man. He is enrolled in journalism school for that purpose. He's my height, when I'm wearing heels, has brown hair and brown eyes, lives not far away in Salisbury, North Carolina. We go out mostly to hit movies, and he explains their appeal afterward, over coffee at a campus hangout. He prides himself on knowing what sells, and why, and what motivates people. Sometimes when we kiss, I imagine he knows exactly what percentage of females close their eyes, and if more males keep theirs open.

I long for Sunny.

Whenever Sunny came to dinner, my father winced at his

surfers' talk and asked him pointedly if he had a "real" name. Harold, Sunny would tell him, and my father would say, that's not such a bad name, you can make Harry out of that, and once he came right out and told Sunny that a man shouldn't have a boy's name.

When Sunny finally joined the Navy my father said, well, they'll make a man out of him.

He's a man, I said, believe me. Look at him and tell me he's not a man. Because Sunny towers over my father, has a Rambo build, and a walk, smile, and way about him that oozes confidence. Hair the color of the sun, deep blue eyes. Always tanned, always. Even my mother murmured, oh, he's a man, Sunny is.

But my father shook his head and said, I don't mean *that*. I mean the boy has a boy's ambition, you only have to listen to all that talk about the big waves, the surf, the beach—either he's a boy or a fish, but he's not someone with his eye on the future. He's not someone thinking about a profession!

One of the hard things about going to college in your hometown is that your family meets your dates right away. If I had the good luck to live in a dorm, my father couldn't cross-examine all of them while I finish dressing and get myself downstairs. Even when I'm ready ahead of time, he manages to squeeze out as much information about them as he can, once he's shaken hands with one, and while we're standing there looking for our exit line.

He likes Alan right away.

After dinner is over, while Alan and I go for a walk, Alan says, "I really like your family. Did they like me, do you think?"

"I know they did."

But my mother never once threw her head back and laughed, the way she used to when Sunny was at the table, never said, oh, *you!* to Alan, like someone trying hard not to love his teasing—no one ever teased her but Sunny.

He'd tell her she looked like Princess Di (maybe . . . a little) and he'd often exclaim, you've made my day, darlin'! when he'd taste her special fried chicken. My father calls her Kate or Mama, and he can't eat anything fried because of the cholesterol, but they've been rocking together on our front porch through twenty years of marriage, and he *does* have a profession: law. He's a judge.

Oh, is he a judge!

Sunny, he said once when Sunny alluded to a future with me. Every Friday noon Marybeth's mother comes down to my office and we go out to lunch. It's a ritual with us: I get to show her off to my colleagues, and we stroll over to the hotel, enjoy an old-fashioned, have the special-of-the-day, and set aside that time just for us. . . . I hope someday my daughter will be going down to her own husband's place of business to do the exact same thing.

Later Sunny said, *He wasn't kidding, was he?*

Him? I said. *Kid?* I said.

It was a week to the day that Sunny asked me to marry him. We were just graduated from high school. I was already planning my courses at the university when Sunny got wind of a job in Santa Monica, running a shop called Sun & Surf. Sunny'd moved from California when his folks broke up. His mom brought him back to Greenville, where she waited table in his grandfather's diner. . . . I never knew what Sunny's father did for a living, but my father, who spent a lot of time trying to worm it out of Sunny, said it sounded as though he was a "common laborer." Can't he be just a laborer? I said. Does he have to be a common one?

Marybeth, said my father, *I'm just looking out for you. I like the boy. He's a nice boy. But we're talking here about the whole picture. . . . Does Sunny ever mention college?*

I want to go to college, I told Sunny.

You can go out on the coast somewhere.

How? Daddy won't pay for it if we get married.

We'll figure out something.

It's too vague, Sunny, and too soon.

What's vague about it?

Don't you want to go to college, Sunny? Don't you want a profession?

Sunny said he couldn't believe I felt the way my father did, in the letter he left with my mother for me. He said the Navy was his best bet, and at least he'd be on water. He didn't say anything about waiting for him, or writing—nothing about the future. I'd said some other things that last night together, after he'd made fun of my father's talk about my parents' Friday-noon ritual. *They don't even touch,* he'd said: *I've never once seen them touch, or heard them use affectionate names, or laugh together. So she shows up at his office once a week—big deal! . . . Honey, we've got a love that'd like to bust through the roof! You don't want to just settle for something like they did! They settled!*

They love each other, I argued back, *it just doesn't show. . . .* Sunny said that was like plastic over wood, and love should splinter, crack, and burn!

You know how it is when someone criticizes your family, even when you might have thought and said the same things.

You strike out when you hear it from another mouth, say things you don't mean, or you do, and wouldn't have said under any other circumstances.

I said, *at least my father could always take care of my mother! At least he'd made something of himself, and she could be proud of him! That's good enough for me,* I said. I knew from the hurt look in Sunny's eyes he was hearing that he wasn't.

"Seventy-four percent of American adults are interested in professional football," Alan says as we walk along under the stars. "Eighty-seven percent of men and sixty-three percent of women."

I can hear Sunny's voice saying *blah blah blah blah blah blah blah!*

"Alan," I say, "what kind of office does an advertising man have?"

"Mine's going to be in New York City, and there'll be a thick rug on the floor, and a view of the whole Manhattan skyline from the windows. Do you like New York, Marybeth?"

"Anyplace but here!" I answer. "I'd like to get out of the South! I'd like to live near an ocean." I was picturing Sunny coming in on a big wave out in California. "I'd like to always be tanned."

Alan shakes his head. "That's out of style now. The ozone layer and all. White skin is in. No one wants a tan anymore."

When we get to the curb, Alan puts his hand under my arm and remarks, "You smell good. What perfume is that?"

"I don't remember what I put on." I was thinking of nights with Sunny we'd walk down this street with our arms wrapped around each other, and Sunny'd say, let's name our kids. Say we have four, two girls and two boys. You get to name a boy and a girl.

Alan lets go of my arm when we get across the street.

"I like the fact you're majoring in economics," he says. "You could go into investment banking. New York is where *you* want to go too."

"Sure, New York," I say. "That's for me."

Next weekend I have a date with John. Premed. Chunky. Beautiful smile. On the porch he tells my father, "I'll take good care of her. Don't worry."

"What are you going to specialize in?" My father gets one last question in as we are heading down the steps.

"Pediatrics, sir," and John grins and grabs my hand as we walk to his white Pontiac.

My mother is sitting in the wicker rocker on the porch, waving at us as we take off.

"Nice people," John says.

We drive to the SAE house with the top down, the moon just rising. "Your family reminds me of mine," he says. "Your mom so warm and welcoming, and your dad all concerned about me. . . . My father's that way about my kid sister when boys come to take her out. I don't have a lot of time to date, so I like dating someone whose family I can meet. You can tell a lot about a girl by her folks."

"They never touch," I tell him. "I mean, not openly."

"Like mine. You watch mine and you wonder how two kids got born."

We look at each other and laugh.

I like him. His wit, his good manners, his dancing, even his "shop talk" about his premed courses. He is a good listener, too, questioning me about what I'm studying, my ideas; he is the perfect date.

"Did you have a good time, sweetheart?" my mother asks.

"So-so." I tell the truth.

"In that case I hate to tell you what's on the hall table."

It's an overnight letter from Western Union. Short and sweet.

ARRIVING TOMORROW NIGHT. HAVE PROFESSION
AND HIGH HOPES. LOVE,

HAROLD.

"He's coming back, isn't he?" Mom says.

I show it to her.

"You like him, Mom, so why did you hate to tell me about this?"

"I like him a lot, but I don't think your father's ever going to resign himself to Sunny, even if he does call himself Harold."

"He has a profession, he says!" I am dancing around the room, hugging the letter. "He has high hopes!"

"I think he's the same old Sunny, honey, and I think it's just going to be more heartbreak. Oh, I *do* like him. Truly I do. But you started seeing Alan and John. You took a step away from Sunny."

"Just give him a chance, Mom."

"Give who a chance?" my father's voice.

He is coming into the living room in his robe and pajamas.

"Harold!" I exclaim. "Just give Harold a chance!"

"We used to chant 'Give peace a chance,' when I was in college," my father says, "and I'd say Sunny having a chance is like peace having a chance. Peace being what it is, and Sunny being what he is, no chance will do much to change things. Won't

23

last. . . . Now, John is a young man I really warm to. Did you have a good time with John?"

"He was the perfect date," I answer.

"You said it was a so-so time," says my mother.

"Maybe I'm not into perfection."

When I meet the little plane that flies from Charlotte to Greenville, I can see Sunny getting off first, lugging his duffel bag, dressed in his Navy uniform, hurrying through the rain, tan as anything, tall, and grinning even before he can spot me in the small crowd.

He has a box of candy—"Not for you, my love," he says, "it's for your mama." Then he kisses me, hugs me, hangs on hard and whispers, "Let's name our kids. Say we've got six, all boys, first one's Harold junior. We could call him Harry."

There is no way I can get him to talk about his profession on the way home in my father's Buick. He says he is going to tell me at the same time he tells my folks, that all we are going to talk about on the way there is how soon I can transfer to the university near the base. He has three more years in the Navy and an application for reduced tuition for Navy wives, providing I still love him the way he loves me, do I? . . . *Yes?* Okay!

He says, "Park the car somewhere fast before we go straight home, because we've got to get the fire burning lower, or we'll scorch your loved ones." Here's a place.

My father growls, "One *hour* getting back here from the airport, was the traffic *that* bad on a weeknight? We thought you'd had an accident. . . ." And my mother purrs, "Guess what's cooking?"

"Fried chicken!" Harold cries, sounding like the same old Sunny. "Darlin', you have made my day! Love you and want some huggin' from my one and only!"

"Oh *you!*" my mother says.

It does not take my father long to start in; he starts in at the same time he picks up his fork.

"What's this about a profession, Sunny? Harold?"

"Yes, sir, I am a professional man now."

"You're becoming a professional sailor, is that it?"

"No, sir. I'm leaving the Navy eventually, but thanks to the Navy, I now have a profession that suits me."

"Which is?"

"I'm an underwater welder."

"Let's eat before we get into all this," says my mother, fast.

"You're a *what*?"

"An underwater welder."

My father begins to sputter about Alan, who is going into advertising, and John, the aspiring baby doctor, those are professions, but what kind of . . . what kind of . . .

And my mother is passing the gravy, passing the cranberry relish, the biscuits, keeping her hands flying between the table and Sunny.

"Where will you, where will . . ." my father again, and if he ever finishes the sentence, I don't know. For I am seeing Sunny see me. I am seeing him be true to me and to himself. Perhaps my father wants to ask where will you do this, where will your office be, for my father is one to think in terms of a man's workplace.

But I am drifting in my thoughts to future Fridays, traditional and loving, donning a wet suit for a rendezvous in the deep blue sea. Keeping my date with that warm fish I married.

SON OF A ONE EYE

Every fall, when it's still hot and people are wearing their summer clothes because the weather hasn't snapped yet, I think of the day we dropped Denny off in the freshman dorm.

My dad wanted to march him right into the Phi Deke fraternity house and say, "Here's your new pledge!"

My mother is the one in the family blessed with some sense of reality, despite the fact that she read us Stephen King as bedtime stories when we were kids. My mother said Denny should stay in the dorm. She said that the fraternity knew about him and they'd invite him over when they were ready. Denny, you see, was a legacy.

What made him a legacy was that Dad had been a Phi Deke when he went to college. If your father was a Phi Deke, the fraternity had to take you. It didn't matter what a legacy looked like, what his grades were, or if he was a dud.

Dad felt good after we left Denny. He said college would teach Denny to assert himself, and the fraternity would make a man out of him. Mom raised her eyebrows and gave me a look. She'd sneaked some of her Crushed Walnut Cake into Denny's garment bag, so I think she knew he was going to need some comfort. Denny had never wanted to go to college, much less join a club there. The poor guy had no defense against Dad's wishes. He never had. To me, a fraternity would seem like a house full of real big brothers. But to Denny, they would be grown-up versions of the ones who'd pushed him around in all the recess yards of his youth.

My heart ached for my big brother, who wasn't big but my size and skinny. A nailbiter, a nerd. Denny was a babbler. People made him so nervous that when he was around them, he described the plots of movies and TV sitcoms. He gnawed at his nails or rubbed one eyebrow so hard with his finger that little hairs fell out.

Dad said he'd outgrow it.

Mom said it was better than the way he was when he was little. Back then, he wouldn't talk at all.

"I can't imagine Denny not talking," I said.

"There was a time," said Dad, "when Denny would only talk to Skipper."

I never knew Skipper well. He'd been Denny's dog. There was an eight-year age difference between Denny and me.

Denny said Skipper wasn't his real name, anyway. His real name was Misery, and he was from the planet of Perfecto, same as Denny.

"Don't laugh, because this is true," Denny would say. He always had something new to add to his story of coming from outer space.

On Perfecto, said Denny, everything was so perfect that

people forgot how to cry. They even had to be reminded there was such a thing as unhappiness. They wore yellow buttons with black sad faces painted on them. And there were crying clubs, something like our comedy clubs. There were tragics performing in them. They'd tell stories that would leave people crying in the aisles.

"You know how here on earth we might name a girl Felicity or Joy?" Denny said. "On Perfecto, they'd call her Sorry or Dismal."

There were times I almost believed Denny's story that he'd invaded my real brother's body before birth. Why *couldn't* there be other forms of life doing research on us? And wouldn't that explain why Denny was so different?

Anyone could tell that Denny wasn't one of the crowd, and it didn't matter what crowd you were talking about. He didn't fit in anywhere, except in his room, where he spent most of his time. There, or in the kitchen watching Mom bake. She made our bread, and our cakes, cookies, and breakfast muffins. He liked watching and thinking up names like Crushed Walnut Cake and Downhearted Doughnuts, Heartsick Cinnamon Rolls, and Weeping White Chocolate Bars. Perfecto names, he told me . . . Shhh—don't tell Mom.

I'd tell Mom anyway. At times I'd get to thinking it would all add, up if there really was a place called Perfecto and Denny was from there.

Mom would say something like, "You go back and tell Denny he'll have a *very* sad story to take back there if he doesn't get his bike out of the driveway before his dad . . . excuse me, *your* dad gets home!"

When Denny wasn't around, our father used to say, "Joey, you got the looks in the family. You're the spitting image of your mom."

Once, I asked him, "What'd Denny get?"

"Hmmm? What'd you say?"

"You heard me," I said. I knew he was stalling, crossing out brains, brawn, and personality. None of it applied to Denny.

But Dad came up with something. "Why, he got that beautiful name," he said. "Dennis Guilder Smith—that's got a ring to it!"

He was right about that. My mother had named Denny. I was named by my father. I was just plain Joe Smith. Not even a middle name. Dad thought middle names, were phony. Thanks, Dad, for all the choices.

Our dad was not imaginative, and he didn't read Stephen King. Dennis Guilder was a character out of a King story about a 1958 Plymouth named Christine.

If Denny had been a girl, guess what name he would have?

Is it easier to be different if you're a boy, or a girl? Would Christine Smith have found people backing away from her as she gave detailed descriptions of *Attack of the Killer Tomatoes* or *Repo Man*?

Postcards from Denny early that autumn were actually Mom's. She had made them out for him ahead of time.

I am feeling a) okay, b) awful, c) in between.

Denny would check all three.

Soon I began wearing sweaters to school, and slipping a blanket over me nights in the top bunk. With Denny gone, I was sleeping up there. I could touch the stars he had pasted to the ceiling so he wouldn't be too lonesome for Perfecto. On Perfecto, the stars were an arm's length away, said Denny, soft as rose petals and the only light.

At the end of September, Dad got tired of postcards that carried no news. He called Denny at college.

"Great! Great!" we heard him say. It was already a suspicious beginning to any conversation between Dad and my brother. When Dad glanced across the room at Mom and me and said, "Denny's got a girlfriend," we both ran for the extensions.

Dad was asking, "How do you like living at Phi Deke?"

"I'm still in the dorm, Dad, until I'm an active member. But I'm treasurer of my pledge class. And I'm taking Mildred to the house for the big Halloween dance."

"Dennis, you don't dance!" said Mom.

"Mildred says dancing bores her anyway, so we'll sit it out in the TV room."

"Where did you meet Mildred?" Mom said. Dad was shouting over her that a man had to learn how to dance and Denny should take lessons.

"The guys fixed me up with her," said Denny. "She was a blind date."

After that, if we wanted to communicate with Denny, we had to call him. All he wanted to talk about was Mildred. Mildred looked like a young Madonna. Mildred was brilliant. Mildred wanted to be a scientist. Mildred believed that our planet was situated in the black hole. Etcetera, etcetera . . . Dad was delighted. He said we could thank the Phi Dekes that finally Denny was finding his way in this world. That's what fraternities were all about, Dad claimed. They gave you confidence, and pointed you where you wanted to go.

The one time Denny did make a call, it was after the Halloween dance.

There wasn't time, he said, to go into detail. But it was a nice dance, he supposed. It had just cost more than he thought it would, which was why he was calling.

I'd never heard Dad okay a request for money so casually. "I bet you all went out to eat, hmmm, that place on the lake costs an arm and a leg, what's the name?"

Denny didn't come up with the name.

Dad said, "A chip off the old block, Den, that's you. When I'd call home from college, you know how my father'd answer the phone? He'd say, 'How much?'"

The night we met Denny at Islip airport for Thanksgiving vacation, he was too tired to talk. Some airline foul-up had made him five hours late. Before we went to bed, he got out this picture of Mildred. It was an 8x10 in an old silver frame. He took the bottom bunk so he could look up at it. He didn't seem to mind that he couldn't reach out and touch the stars. All Denny wanted to talk about was Mildred. He said she looked like a young Madonna.

"How do you like the Phi Dekes?" Dad asked him at breakfast.

"They aren't going to make me an active, Dad."

"They have to, Son, like it or lump it."

"Not if you break a trust. Just listen, Dad. Okay?"

Denny told us that Mildred had been workings her way through college. She clerked at a mall just outside Ithaca. She had some scholarship money, too, but everything was more expensive than she'd thought. She was struggling to survive at all.

"She was very impressed that I was a Phi Deke pledge." Denny said. "So the night of the dance I bragged about being treasurer of the pledge class. While everyone was dancing, I showed her the president's suite, where the safe was. I told her the combination was the date that Christopher Columbus discovered America."

"1492," I said. I was pleased that I could remember any date, since I'd never gotten higher than *C* in history.

But Mom was way ahead of the story. She held her head with her hands and murmured, "Oh, no, Denny."

"She couldn't help it," my brother said. "It was like showing a baby where candy was. There was about two hundred dollars cash in the safe. We were watching TV downstairs later and she excused herself to go to the john. That's when she went back up and cleaned us out."

"Did you pay back the money?"

"Yes. Some of it I borrowed from you, Dad."

"Then they ought to give you a second chance. You're a legacy!"

"They won't, and I don't want them to," said Denny. "I didn't think I belonged there and I don't—not in a fraternity, not in college at all. I think I might be a writer."

"And starve to death," Dad added. But he wasn't going to give Denny a fight this time. Not even Dad would send Denny back into the fray after he'd made such a valiant effort at college, and romance, and frat life.

Mom just put her arms around Denny and said she was so sorry. Did he know where Mildred was?

Denny said he didn't care. After that, he never talked about her. But for a long time he kept her picture on the bureau. She would smile at us in our room, making me feel sad for my brother.

Maybe Denny listened too well to Dad about starving to death if he became a writer. Instead, Denny got a job in a bakery. By the time I was a junior in high school, he had borrowed enough from the bank to buy the place.

The Perfecto Bakery does okay with its Teardrop Cookies, Heartbreak Bread, and Glum Pudding. And you'd have to say that Denny does okay, too. He lives alone above the bakery in an apartment. He sleeps in our old bunk bed, which Mom gave him after I was graduated. He sleeps in the top bunk, I know, because he has put stars up on the ceiling in his bedroom.

As "D.G. Smith," he has not written very much. Denny takes a long time getting his ideas down just the way he wants them. Two of his stories have been published in *Fantasy* magazine, and reprinted in anthologies. One was translated into French. He has some small fame because of them, even though he was paid very little.

The first is about Perfecto, as Denny described it to me over the years.

But it is the second one I find most interesting. That one is about a club of the One Eyes. The One Eyes are male inhabitants of Pitch Dark, a place inside the black hole. Any Son of a One Eye is invited to join, unless he is proven to be dishonorable. One of the legacies has two eyes. His name is

Guilder. Not only is he ugly with his two eyes, but his mind cannot stay on one subject only, as the minds of Pitch Darks do. His mind runs all over the place, and he is repulsive because of it.

Shortly after he is put in charge of The One Eyes' Heavy Egg, he meets the beautiful Muldred. Unable to believe that this lovely one-eyed female with the narrow mind might find him attractive, he boasts of guarding The Heavy Egg. He tells her how to get it out from the glass case. She takes it from the clubhouse, leaving Guilder to resign in disgrace. When he learns from an enemy of the One Eyes that Muldred was paid six rare scarlet parrot feathers to lure Guilder into disgrace, he still keeps a likeness of her in his locket. Across it he's written ONLY TRUST YOURSELF.

Mom said that Denny's stories always have a kernel of truth in them. She said that Perfecto is really about a kid who's so offbeat he feels as though he's from another planet . . . And we know who the One Eyes are, don't, we? said Mom. She said that after she read the second story, she had asked Denny if he'd known when he was home Thanksgiving that the Phi Dekes had set him up. My brother told her that Mildred had left him a note confessing everything. At the end, she had written: *I don't blame, you if you never trust anyone again!*

Dad said he didn't believe it. Either the girl was a liar, or Denny was twisting the truth because he was still mad at Phi Deke. "Don't listen to your brother on the subject of Phi Deke," Dad told me that last summer before I left home.

"Denny never mentions Phi Deke," I said. He never mentioned Mildred, either.

"Your brother Dennis has a great imagination, I'll give him that," Dad had said. "But where will that get you in the real world?"

No one at the Phi Deke house remembers hearing anything about a Dennis Guilder Smith. Not even the housemother who remembers pledges from way back in the 1970s.

I took the trouble to find out that the, treasurer of the pledge class that year was not named Smith, but Langhorn . . . Denny's name isn't on record anywhere. It's as though my brother was never even there.

THE AUTHOR

Before the author comes to school, we all have to write him, saying we are glad he is coming and we like his books.

That is Ms. Terripelli's idea. She is our English teacher and she was the one who first got the idea to have real, live authors visit Leighton Middle School.

She wants the author to feel welcome.

You are my favorite author, I write.

I have never read anything he's written.

Please send me an autographed picture, I write. I am sure this will raise my English grade, something I need desperately, since it is not one of my best subjects.

The truth is: I have best friends and best clothes and best times, but not best subjects.

I am going to be an author, too, someday, I write, surprised to see the words pop up on the screen. But I am writing on the computer in the school library and there is something wonderful about the way any old thought can become little green letters in seconds, which you can erase with one touch of your finger.

I don't push WordEraser, however.

I like writing that I am going to be an author.

The person I am writing to is Peter Sand.

My name happens to be Peter too.

Peter Sangetti.

I might shorten my name to Peter Sang, when I become an author, I write. *Then maybe people will buy my books by mistake, thinking they are getting yours. (Ha! Ha!)*

Well, I write, *before this turns into a book and you sell it for money, I will sign off, but I will be looking for you when you show up at our school.*

I sign it *Sincerely,* although that's not exactly true.

The night before the author visit, my dad comes over to see me. My stepfather and my mother have gone off to see my stepbrother, Tom, in Leighton High School's version of *The Sound of Music.*

To myself, and sometimes to my mother, I call him Tom Terrific. Naturally, he has the lead in the musical. He is Captain Von Trapp. If they ever make the Bible into a play, he will be God.

I like him all right, but I am tired of playing second fiddle to him always. He is older, smarter, and better looking, and his last name is Prince. Really.

I can't compete with him.

It's funny, because the first words out of my dad's mouth that night are, "I can't compete with that."

He is admiring the new CD audio system my stepfather had ordered from the Sharper Image catalog. It is an Aiwa with built-in BBE sound.

"It's really for Tom Terrific," I say, but it is in the living room, not Tom's bedroom, and Dad knows my CD collection is my pride and joy.

I suppose just as I try to compete with Tom Terrific, my dad tries to compete with Thomas Prince, Sr. . . . Both of us are losing the game, it seems. My dad is even out of work just now, although it is our secret . . . not to be shared with my mom or stepfather.

The plant where he worked was closed. He'd have to move out of the state to find the same kind of job he had there, and he doesn't want to leave me.

"I'm not worried about you," I lie. And then I hurry to change the subject, and tell him about the author's visit, next day.

He smiles and shakes his head. "Funny. I once wanted to be a writer."

"I never knew that."

"Sure. One time I got this idea for a story about our cat. She was always sitting in the window of our apartment building, looking out. She could never get out, but she'd sit there, and I'd think it'd be her dream come true if she could see a little of the world! Know what I mean, Pete?"

"Sure I do." I also know my dad always wished he could travel. He is the only person I've ever known who actually reads *National Geographic.*

He laughs. "So I invented a story about the day she got out. Here was her big chance to run around the block!"

"What happened?"

"A paper bag fell from one of the apartments above ours. It landed right on Petunia's head. She ran around the block, all right, but she didn't see a thing."

Both of us roar at the idea, but deep down I don't think it is that hilarious, considering it is my dad who dreamed it up.

What's he think—that he'll never see the world? Never have his dreams come true?

"Hey, what's the matter?" he says. "You look down in the dumps suddenly."

"Not me," I say.

"Aw, that was a dumb story," he says. "Stupid!"

"It was fine," I say.

"No, it wasn't," he says. "I come over here and say things to spoil your evening. You'd rather hear your music."

"No, I wouldn't," I say, but he is getting up to go.

We are losing touch not living in the same house anymore.

Whenever I go over to his apartment, he spends a lot of time apologizing for it. It is too small. It isn't very cheerful. It needs a woman's touch. I want to tell him that if he'd just stop pointing out all the things wrong with it, I'd like it fine . . . but it is turning out that we aren't great talkers anymore. I don't say everything on my mind anymore.

He shoots me a mock punch at the door and tells me that next week he'll get some tickets to a hockey game. Okay with me? I say he doesn't have to, thinking of the money, and he says I know it's not like going to the World Series or anything. I'd gone to the World Series the year before with my stepfather.

"Let up," I mumble.

"What?" he says.

"Nothing."

He says, "I heard you, Pete. You're right. You're right."

Next day, waiting for me out front is Ms. Terripelli.

"He asked for you, Pete! You're going to be Mr. Sand's guide for the day."

"Why me?" I ask.

"Because you want to be a writer?" She looks at me and I look at her.

"Oh, that," I say.

"You never told the class that," she says.

"It's too personal."

"Do you write in secret, Pete?"

"I have a lot of ideas," I say.

"Good for you!" says Ms. Terripelli, and she hands me a photograph of Peter Sand. It is autographed. It also has written on it, "Maybe someday I'll be asking for yours, so don't change your name. Make me wish it was mine, instead."

"What does all that mean?" Ms. Terripelli asks me.

"Just author stuff," I say.

I put the picture in my locker and go to the faculty lounge to meet him.

He is short and plump, with a mustache. He looks like a little colonel of some sort, because he has this booming voice and a way about him that makes you feel he knows his stuff.

"I never write fantasy," he says. "I write close to home. When you read my books, you're reading about something that happened to me! . . . Some authors write both fantasy and reality!"

At the end of his talks he answers all these questions about his books and he autographs paperback copies.

I hang out with him the whole time.

We don't get to say much to each other until lunch.

The school doesn't dare serve him what we get in the cafeteria, so they send out for heros, and set up a little party for him in the lounge.

The principal shows up, and some librarians from the Leighton Town Library.

When we do get a few minutes to talk he asks me what I am writing.

I say, "We had this cat, Petunia, who was always looking out the window . . ."

He is looking right into my eyes as though he is fascinated, and I finish the story.

"Wow!" he says. "Wow!"

"It's sort of sad," I say.

"It has heart and it has humor, Pete," he says. "The best stories always do."

His last session is in the school library, and members of the town are invited.

About fifty people show up.

He talks about his books for a while, and then he starts talking about me.

He tells the story about Petunia. He called it wistful and amusing, and he says anyone who can think up a story like that knows a lot about the world already.

I get a lot of pats on the back afterward, and Ms. Terripelli says, "Well, you've had quite a day for yourself, Pete."

By this time I am having trouble looking her in the eye.

Things are a little out of hand, but what the heck—he is on his way to the airport and back to Maine, where he lives. What did it hurt that I told a few fibs?

Next day, the *Leighton Lamplighter* has the whole story. I hadn't even known there was a reporter present. There is the same photograph Peter Sand has given to me, and there is my name in the article about the author visit.

My name. Dad's story of Petunia, with no mention of Dad.

"Neat story!" says Tom Terrific.

My stepfather says if I show him a short story all finished and ready to send out somewhere, he'll think about getting me a word processor.

"I don't write for gain," I say.

Mom giggles. "You're a wiseguy, Pete."

"Among other things," I say.

Like a liar, I am thinking. Like a liar and a cheat.

When Dad calls, I am waiting for the tirade.

He has a bad temper. He is the type who leaves nothing unsaid when he blows. I expect him to blow blue: he does when he loses his temper. He comes up with slang that would knock the socks off the Marine Corps.

"Hey, Pete," he says, "you really liked my story, didn't you?"

"Too much, I guess. That's why you didn't get any credit."

"What's mine is yours, kid. I've always told you that."

"I went off the deep end, I guess, telling him I want to be a writer."

"An apple never falls far from the tree, Pete. That was my ambition when I was your age."

"Yeah, you told me. . . . But *me*. What do I know?"

"You have a good imagination, son. And you convinced Peter Sand what you were saying was true."

"I'm a good liar, I guess."

"Or a good storyteller. . . . Which one?"

Why does he have to say which one?

Why does he have to act so pleased to have given me something?

The story of Petunia isn't really a gift. I realize that now. It was more like a loan.

I can tell the story, just as my dad told it to me, but when I try to turn myself from a liar into a storyteller, it doesn't work on paper.

I fool around with it for a while. I try.

The thing is: fantasy is not for me.

I finally find out what is when I come up with a first sentence which begins:

Before the author comes to school, we all have to write him, saying we are glad he is coming and we like his books.

You see, I am an author who writes close to home.

WE MIGHT AS WELL
ALL BE STRANGERS

It was Christmas," said my grandmother, "and I went from the boarding school in Switzerland with my roommate, to her home in Germany.

"She was afraid it would not be grand enough for me there . . . that because my family lived in New York, it would seem too modest, and she kept saying, 'We live very simply,' and she kept saying, 'Except for my uncle Karl, who pays my tuition, we are not that rich.'

"I told her no, no, this is thrilling to me, and I meant it. Everywhere there was Christmas: wreaths of *Tannenbaum* hung, the Christmas markets were still open in the little towns we passed through. Every house had its *Christbaum*—a tall evergreen with a star on top.

"I was not then a religious Jew. I was a child from a family that did not believe in religion . . . and what I felt was envy, and joy at the activity: the Christmas-card landscape, snow falling, smoke rising from chimneys, and villagers rushing through the streets with gift-wrapped packages, and the music of Christmas.

"Then we saw the signs outside her village.

"*Juden unerwünscht.* (Jews not welcome.)

"And other, smaller signs, saying things in German like kinky hair and hooked noses not wanted here, and worse, some so vile I can't say them to you.

"'These have nothing to do with us,' Inge said. 'These are just political, to do with this new chancellor, Hitler. Pay no attention, Ruth.'

"I did not really even think of myself as a Jew, and while I was shocked, I did not take it personally since I was from America. We even had our own Christmas tree when I was a tiny child. . . . Now I was *your* age, Alison. Sixteen.

"Her parents rushed out to greet us, and welcome us. Inside there was candlelight and mistletoe and wonderful smells of food cooking, and we were hungry after the long trip. The house was filled with the family, the little children dressed up, everyone dressed up and joyous.

"We sat around a huge table, and wine was served to the adults, and Inge's mother said we girls could have half a glass ourselves. We felt grown-up. We sipped the wine and Christmas carols played over the radio, but there was so much talk, it was like a thin sound of the season with in front of us the tablecloth, best china, crystal glasses! I thought, What does she mean she lives modestly? There were servants . . . and it looked like a little house from the outside only. Inside it was big and lively, with presents under the tree we would open later. I was so impressed and delighted to be included.

"Then a maid appeared and in a sharp voice said, 'Frau Kantor? There is something I must say.'

"Inge's mother looked annoyed. 'What *is* it?'

"Then this thin woman in her crisp white uniform with

the black apron said, 'I cannot serve the food. I do not hand food to a man, woman, or child'—her eyes on me suddenly—'of Jewish blood ever again.'"

My grandmother paused and shook her head.

I said, "What happened then?"

"Then," my grandmother said, "we carried our plates into the kitchen and served ourselves. . . . All except for Inge's uncle Karl, who left because he had not known until that moment that I was Inge's *Jewish* friend from her school."

"I never heard that you were there when all of that was going on, Grandma."

"It was my one and only time in Germany," she said. "So you don't have to tell me about what it feels like to be an outsider. You don't have to tell me about prejudice. But Alison, I thank you for telling me about yourself. I'm proud that you told me first."

A week later, my mother said, "Why do you have to *announce* it, Alison?"

"Is that all you're going to say?"

"No, that's first. First I'm going to say there was no need to announce it. You think I don't know what's going on with you and Laura? I don't need eyes in the back of my head to figure that out."

"But it makes you uncomfortable to *hear* it from me, is that it?"

"I can't do anything about it, can I? I see it every time you bring her here. I would like to believe it's a stage you're going through, but from what I've read and heard, it isn't."

"No. It isn't."

"I can kiss grandchildren good-bye, I guess, if you persist with this choice."

"Mom, it's not a choice. Was it a choice when you fell in love with Dad?"

"Most definitely. I chose him!"

"What I mean is—you didn't choose him over a woman."

"I would never choose a woman, Alison! Never! Life is family. Or I *used* to think it was. Before *this*!"

"What I mean is—there were only males you were attracted to."

"Absolutely! Where you got this—it wasn't from *me.*"

"So what if the world was different, and men loved men and women loved women, but you were still *you*? What would you do?"

My mother shrugged. "Find another world, I guess."

"So that's what *I* did. I found another world."

"Good! Fine! You have your world and I have mine. Mine happens to be the *real* world, but never mind. You always went your own way."

Then she sighed and said, "I'm only glad your father's not alive to hear his favorite daughter tell him she's *gay.*"

"I was his *only* daughter, Mother."

"All the more reason. . . . We dreamed of the day you'd bring our grandchildren to us."

"That's still an option. I may bring a grandchild to you one day."

"Don't."

"Don't?"

"Not if it's one of those test-tube/artificial-insemination children. I'm talking about a real child, a child of our blood, with a mother *and* a father. I don't care to have one of those kids I see on Donahue who was made with a turkey baster or some other damn thing! Alison, what you've gotten yourself involved in is not just a matter of me saying Oh, so you're *gay*, fine, and then life goes on. What you've gotten yourself involved in is *serious*!"

"That's why I'm telling you about it."

"That's not why you're telling me about it!"

"Why am I telling you about it?"

"You want me to say it's okay with me. You gays want the whole world to say it's okay to be gay!"

"And it isn't."

"No, it is *not*! Okay? I've said how I feel! You are what you are, okay, but it is not okay with me what you are!"

"So where do we go from here?"

"I'll tell you where not to go! Don't go to the neighbors, and don't go to my friends, and don't go to your grandmother!"

"What do you think Grandmother would say?"

"When she stopped weeping?"

"You think she'd weep?"

"Alison," my mother said, "it would *kill* your grandmother!"

"You think Grandma wouldn't understand?"

"I *know* Grandmother wouldn't understand! What is to understand? She has this grandchild who'll never bring her great-grandchildren."

"I might bring her some straight from the Donahue show."

"Very funny. *Very* funny," my mother said. Then she said, "Alison, this coming-out thing isn't working. You came out to me, all right, I'm your mother and maybe you had to come out to me. But where your grandmother's concerned: Keep quiet."

"You think she'd want that?"

"I think she doesn't even *dream* such a thing could come up! She's had enough *tsuris* in life. Back in the old country there were relatives lost in the Holocaust! Isn't that enough for one woman to suffer in a lifetime?"

"Maybe that would make her more sympathetic."

"Don't compare gays with Jews—there's no comparison."

"I'm both. There's prejudice against both. And I didn't choose to be either."

"If you want to kill an old woman before her time, tell her."

"I think you have Grandmother all wrong."

"If I have Grandmother all wrong," said my mother, "then I don't know her and you don't know me, and we might as well all be strangers."

"To be continued," I wrote in my diary that night.

My grandmother knew . . . my mother knew . . . one day my mother would know that my grandmother knew.

All coming-out stories are a continuing process.

Strangers take a long time to become acquainted, particularly when they are from the same family.

LIKE FATHER, LIKE SON

Maybe you'd like us to call you something else," my father said to Harley.

"Why?" Harley said. "Because it was a Harley my folks were riding when they were killed?"

"I know your real name's Ken Jr. I just thought—"

Harley waved away the suggestion. "I'm used to my nickname," he told my dad. "Anyway, it wasn't the Harley that killed them. They'd been celebrating their anniversary at Jungle Pete's, and Pop probably couldn't even see the road."

"OK. Harley it is!"

And Harley it was. In my room, while I slept on the sunporch hide-a-bed. Riding my 10-speed bike. Wearing my socks, my jackets. Playing my CDs, and hogging my PC. Harley made himself right at home.

"That's what we want him to do," my father said. "It won't be for long, Connor. His uncle's going to take him as soon as he finishes his work in Alaska. If it wasn't for Harley's dad, I wouldn't be alive."

Dad wasn't that surprised when he saw the swastika Harley had pinned to his cap the day we met his bus.

All Dad said was, "Better take that off, Harley. That won't go over too well here in Cortland."

"It's just a decoration—doesn't mean anything," said Harley, but he unfastened it and stuck it in his pocket.

The reason Dad wasn't surprised was that he'd been through the Gulf War with Harley's father, and he said Ken Sr. was a little "insensitive" too.

That was putting it mildly. After the war, he'd call Dad long distance and he'd always start off the conversation with the kind of jokes Dad hated: Polish jokes, jokes about Jews, blacks, Italians—no race or color was excluded.

If I ever told a joke like that, I'd be grounded, and Dad didn't have any buddies who spoke that way either. But Ken McFarland always got away with it.

"That's just Ken," Dad said. "He doesn't know any better. But he knew how to pull me out of the back of that Bradley when we got hit. He risked his life doing it, too!"

Both Dad and McFarland were reservists who suddenly found themselves in Iraq back when Saddam marched into Kuwait . . . I was still in middle school then, wearing a yellow ribbon and an American flag, running to the mailbox every day, and never missing a Sunday in church.

I didn't dislike Harley. He was friendly and so polite my mother kept commenting on his good manners. We all felt real bad about his folks' death too, and we couldn't do enough for him.

But there were times, a lot of times, when my mother'd tell him at the dinner table, "We don't call people that, Harley." Or, "Harley? We don't think so much about a person's race or color."

He'd say, "Sorry, M'am. I don't have anything against any-one. I'm just kidding around."

"But I have a problem with it, Harley," Mom would try, "and it sounds like you *are* prejudiced when you talk that way."

"Not me," Harley'd tell her, always with this big smile he has, his blue eyes twinkling.

"Cork it around here!" Dad would say.

"Yes, sir. Right. I'll watch it," would come the answer. But there seemed to be no way he could stop himself. It was built-in . . . Sometimes after my folks called him on it, they would roll their eyes to the ceiling, ready to give up on trying to change him . . . I made up my mind I wasn't going to lose any sleep over it. He'd be gone soon.

He was a fish out of water in Cortland. He'd come in sum-mer. I had a job waiting tables at Tumble Inn. Mom and Dad worked too, so Harley was home by himself a lot watching TV, playing computer games, riding my bike around. He was 15, as I was, and he didn't have a lot of money, but Dad said let him have the summer off: Poor guy. Let him do what he wanted. He was going through enough.

He never showed that he was going through anything. He put a photograph of his parents out on my bureau, and he ran up our phone bills calling his buddies. He'd tell them eventually he was going to live with his uncle in Wisconsin. ("Yeah, I *know* it sucks!") And he'd ask a lot of questions about what was going on. Then he'd tell jokes like his father'd told—we'd hear him in my room hooting and howling, spewing the same kind of language my folks had called him on.

His uncle's job in Alaska took longer than we'd thought,

and I dreaded it when I heard he was going to school with me come September.

Dad said he'd find his own crowd—let him be, so I let him be. I told kids I hung out with how his father had saved my dad's life, and what happened to his folks, and then I let him fend for himself.

Harley was really smart, and that surprised me. But he wasn't good at making friends. It was hard to be a new guy, too. We all knew each other since grade school.

Teachers warned Harley about his racist language. He always seemed surprised, and always protested that he was just kidding around. He *was* funny when he told his kind of jokes. The kids laughed at the accents he'd come up with, but he made them feel uncomfortable, too . . . I'd just walk away, embarrassed for him, I guess . . . and embarrassed he was staying with us.

I'd see him sitting by himself in the cafeteria, looking around at everyone in groups. Once I felt sorry for him, and went over to sit with him. But he said, "You better get back to your crowd." I didn't ask him to join us. I knew he'd say something that would either trigger a fight or hurt someone's feelings. My father called him a "loose cannon," and I think that was why we didn't invite the neighbors over for our usual backyard barbecues.

He was a little guy: short for his age and he said he wasn't into sports. He didn't take to the roughneck wise guys he might have got along with better, if he'd made any effort. They ignored him, too.

I'd stayed on at Tumble Inn, after school started, working afternoons setting up tables, and weekend nights I was in the dining room. Harley was by himself a lot.

•   •   •

Don't ask me why Jitz Rossi got it into his head to go after him, but he did. It happened on a Saturday morning when Harley and I were walking back from town after helping Mom load the groceries into her Pinto. She had other errands—it was a great fall day—and we decided to head back home along Highland Avenue.

Jitz was waiting for us at the top of the hill. He had his own Harley, and he was sitting on it, with a red-and-white bandanna around his forehead, a leather vest, and bikers' gloves . . . A few of his buddies were behind him on their bikes.

The funny thing was Jitz wasn't that different from Harley. He was a lot bigger (star of the wrestling team), but he had the same "insensitivity," as my father'd put it. He was a bully, though, and I think what got him going was that he figured Harley's style was too much like his.

There was that nickname, too. That might have caught Jitz's attention.

The first thing Jitz said was, "How come you call yourself Harley?"

"It's my name."

"Where's your Harley?"

"I don't got one!" Harley laughed. "Got the name without the game."

"I hear you got a name for Italians, too," Jitz said. "I hear you're an outsider with a smart mouth."

Harley said, "I hear it only takes two people to bury your relatives, because there's only two handles on a garbage can."

What I remember after that little crack was Jitz getting off his Harley in perfect sync with the guys behind him. It looked like some kind of orchestrated ballet.

Next, this big bruiser had me down on the ground, slamming my head against the dirt.

What I didn't know was that Harley was a Karate expert, and that there was more power in his small frame and tiny hands than there was in all four of the bikers who went after us. He took them on one by one, starting with Jitz, and then the guy holding me down.

After they all hobbled back on their bikes and roared off, Harley brushed the grass and dirt off me and grinned.

My head and back felt wrecked and I had a nosebleed.

"Where would you dumb Micks be without the McFarlands to pull you out of tanks and up off your butts?" he said.

He was laughing and slapping his knee, and he didn't see my punch coming.

His body jerked back and one hand grabbed his jaw, and he looked at me wide-eyed. "What the HECK?" he said. "What's *that* for? I just saved your butt, Connor!"

"That," I shouted back at him, "is for making it necessary to save my butt!"

"You mad because I called you a dumb Mick?"

"I'm mad because we've been tip-toeing around trying to tell you you're this stupid toilet mouth! We hate the things you say! My dad hated your dad's dumb jokes. Every time he called my dad wanted to plug his ears!"

"My old man saved your dad's life!"

"Are we supposed to pay for that forever? When we go home, *you* get the hide-a-bed! Stop wearing my jacket. Put your dumb swastika back on and stay clear of me!"

I was starting down the hill, and Harley was following after me. "Why didn't you say something?"

"We *did* say something!"

"Your mom and dad did. You never did!"

"I was trying to be nice because your folks died!"

"But *you* know I just kid around, Connor."

"From now on kid around somewhere else! I don't need my head banged in the dirt because you're this bigot!"

"You should have said something before."

"I'm saying it now! Get it? You're an embarrassment! You don't have a brain in your thick head!"

"An *embarrassment*?" He sounded really amazed. "I embarrass you?" He was trailing behind me, his voice suddenly a few registers higher than usual.

"That's right, and my family, too. You sound ignorant."

"I'm smarter than you. My grades are higher than yours."

That was true. He always made all As. I said, "Yeah, but we can't take you anyplace with that mouth of yours. You're not fit. You sound like you crawled out of some gutter."

I don't know what else I said. I guess I said a lot of petty stuff, too, about him wearing my socks and using my PC too much. I just kept babbling away because of the pain I felt. I was finally tired of holding everything in, walking around on eggshells so as not to offend The Great Filth Mouth.

When I got home from work that night, he was in bed on the sleeping porch. His parents' photograph was out there with him on the wicker table near the alarm clock.

I told Dad what happened and he said, "I'm not surprised. Ken knew Karate too . . . But Harley's right. You should have said something before this. We owe that to friends, if we want to keep them for friends. *I* should have told Ken, instead of dreading our phone talks. We could have become real friends, but I missed that chance because I was too chicken to just say knock it off . . . Now that you've cooled down, maybe you have more to say to Harley."

The next day my folks went to church. I stayed home purposely. I was making breakfast in the kitchen when Harley walked in.

He hadn't expected to find me there. His eyes looked away from mine, and he was ready to head back into the living room when I said, "Want some eggs?"

"I got one on my chin," he murmured, "thanks to you."

"Nothing like they've all got. You're a good fighter."

"I guess with my big mouth I'd *better* be. Right, Connor?"

He folded his hands across his chest and gave me this sheepish grin.

"Right!" I agreed.

"OK?" he said, and then quickly he said, "I'll make us toast. I can do that."

End of discussion, and we never spoke of it again.

Harley didn't make another slip after that.

He wouldn't move back into my bedroom, even though I told him we should take turns. I thought Jitz Rossi would want to even up the score, but instead he tried to get him on the wrestling team since we needed to beat Ithaca, the all-time champions . . . Harley said he only went in for the martial arts. They weren't big at Cortland High.

Finally, his uncle got back and sent for him.

A month after he left, I got a postcard from Madison.

All it said was, "Thanks, Connor."

I keep wishing I hadn't said all that stuff about him giving me back my room and not taking my socks etcetera. I keep remembering how he took his folks' photograph out to the sleeping porch the first night he spent there. And I can't forget that Sunday morning. I'd feel better if I'd told him calmly what I'd hollered at him in anger.

I should have had the guts to say more.

Maybe he got it, finally . . . or maybe someone in Wisconsin will do him a favor and level with him.

But maybe not, too. And that's what keeps me awake some nights.

I WILL NOT THINK OF MAINE

You'd think he'd be pale, that he'd come from the shadows, that I'd never see him very clearly, but Maine stepped into the kitchen on a sunny Saturday morning looking the same way he always did.

So I said, "I must be dreaming."

I'd dreamed he'd come back maybe a dozen times since his death, but it had been months since I'd had that dream.

In it he always looked sad. He always said, "I'm so sorry, Zoë. I didn't mean to go that way."

"You couldn't help it," I'd say. "You were so wild, Maine. You weren't like other kids."

Then I'd wake up. I'd feel full of him again. I'd remember how he stood across my room in the dream, with his long hair and his beautiful face, the one skull earring he always wore, the tattoo of the white pinecone and tassel on his arm, the blue-and-white sweatband on his forehead, like the blue and white of his eyes. I'd remember the low purr of his chuckle when something pleased him.

"I dreamed of Maine again," I'd tell my brother.

"Forget Maine, will you, please? He nearly killed Daddy."

Then there he was in our kitchen one summer morning, big as life. Nothing about him said death. "Are you a ghost, Maine?"

He laughed hard, but it was not a happy sound, not like another boy's laughter. He slapped his knee where his jeans were torn, his hands filled with rings, those silver bracelets he liked jangling down one arm.

He said, "We don't use the word 'ghost.' We don't haunt houses or that sort of thing. We call ourselves revenants."

"I never heard that word."

"A revenant is someone who comes back."

Then he did what he always used to do, and it would make my mother furious. He opened the refrigerator door, reached in for the carton of orange juice, put it up to his lips, tossed his head back, and took a long gulp.

"I can't believe it's really you," I finally said.

"Your loving pretend brother is back. Am I your dream come true, Zoë?"

"I guess." I was a little embarrassed to admit it. I *had* thought of him that way. But even though Maine and I weren't related, my family had adopted him, and called him "Son." So now I had two brothers.

My family would never have let me date Maine Foremann under any circumstances, not just because he was family. But also because he was different from other boys. He looked like some dark, edgy character out of an old English novel filled with moors and dungeons.

Back then girls hung out in groups nights, often colliding with boys who did the same.

I could never think of anything to say.

The boys weren't big conversationalists, either.

My mother used to say, "Don't you know why Nelson Rider calls you up all the time, Zoë? He's trying to find the words to ask you out."

"All he talks about is acting in the school plays."

"Invite him over. You'll see."

"What would we do?"

"What do you do when you spend time with Maine?"

"That's different," I said. "I always know what to say to Maine."

The truth was, we hadn't talked that much. But I felt close to him. I felt in some secret way he had the same feeling about me, even though he never said so. I looked out at life through my big thick glasses and waited for things to change.

I was always a major daydreamer, even losing track of what went on in movies I'd watch, because I was thinking of what I'd say one day when Maine came into the theater and just sat down in the empty seat next to me.

Maybe I'd say, "What are you doing here?"

Maybe he'd say, "Well, I knew you were in here so I bought a ticket."

And I'd say . . . never mind what I'd say, or what he'd say. If I had all the hours back I'd spent daydreaming about that sort of thing, I'd be the same age I was then. Thirteen. That was my style, age thirteen. I was waiting for Maine to speak up, and tell me what was in his heart.

Mostly, Maine hung out with my real brother, Carl.

They were both fifteen and neither one was that interested in girls yet.

They liked skateboarding together. They'd go over to Heartsunk Hill and show off. Carl said Maine was a daredevil, so much so sometimes Carl thought he was a little crazy. He said it with a tone of admiration, mostly, but occasionally he sounded exasperated, as though Maine had gone too far . . . like the time Maine brought some beer home he'd gotten an older boy to buy for him. My folks were down at the movies.

He'd shrugged and said, "Your mom doesn't like me drinking your orange juice so I brought my own refreshments."

Carl told him, "You can drink our orange juice, just don't drink from the container. Put it in a glass."

"I've got my own drink now."

"Don't drink it here or I'll be grounded," Carl said.

Maine had a six-pack with him.

He drank it out in the backyard hammock, singing songs by himself. He got louder and sillier, and the cats ran inside and hid under the bed, and the dog wouldn't stop barking at him.

Then he got really sick. I never saw anyone so sick and sorry, and when my folks got back my father had to put him to bed.

Neither of my folks stayed mad at him. Next day, Mom just said, "That boy is so lost, Zoë. I don't know if we're enough to make up for all that's happened to him. But you're a good sister to him, honey."

"I don't think of him as my brother," I said.

She changed the subject. "Carl says Nelson Rider's in the school play."

"When isn't he? He calls me up and says things like 'Boy, is my part hard! I've got more lines than anyone.' What am I supposed to say to that?"

"Say, 'Congratulations!' Or say, 'Tell me about the play.'"

"We're all going to see the play, so I'll know what it's about soon."

"What would you say if Maine said, 'Boy, is my part hard!'?"

"Maine wouldn't be in a school play," I said. "That's not his style."

"Oh, I saw his style last night. Your father and I came along right in time for the upchucking."

"That's not fair," I said. "And Nelson Rider's ears stick out."

Maine seemed so innocent when he'd sit with me and tell me things he'd like to do someday. He'd say he was going back to Maine where he was born, and he was going to live in the woods near a cliff overlooking the ocean.

None of the other boys at school liked Maine. He'd come to us in his freshman year when his parents moved to our town. He'd never connected with a crowd. He shaved his whole head once and painted a Happy face on top, with tears dropping from its eyes. He made no effort to get better than passing grades, even though he knew the answers to most every question any teacher asked in class. He'd tell us school bored him. He complained he missed the weather in Bangor, where he used to live. He missed the bitter cold. Even in freezing weather he wouldn't wear gloves or a scarf, or ear-muffs like the rest of us.

In falling snow I'd see him with his jacket open, shirt unbuttoned, boots laced only halfway—he had a flair. I envied him that. My mother told me flair and fashion didn't just *happen*—you had to create it for yourself. You had to work at it.

I always doubted there was much I could do with myself. I threw on my clothes and tried not to look in a mirror because I'd see that I was hopeless.

One day, when the family was new in town, Maine's mother showed up at our house looking for him. She was beautiful, and she was driving this white Porsche convertible, and she said, "Tell him his father and I are going to California tonight and we'd like to see him before we go."

Maine could hear her. He was hiding in the hall closet.

When she left, I said, "Wow! Is that your mom? Was that her car?"

Maine said, "You're very impressionable, Zoë."

Carl said, "What do they do in California?"

"They sun themselves," Maine said.

"What does your father do for a living?"

"He makes movies," Maine said.

"Wow!" I said.

"Really?" Carl asked.

"Horror movies," he said. "B movies. . . . You'd think he didn't have a brain in his head."

"But she looks so glitzy, Maine, and she's nice!"

"I'm not close to them. They're always gone."

"Do you ever go with them?" I asked.

"I prefer not to be seen with them," said Maine.

He'd break me up saying things like that. He was cool. I always wanted to be like that: cool.

That morning he showed up in our kitchen, Maine said, "I came back for a reason, Zoë."

"To say you're sorry for almost running over my father? He was in the hospital for months, and he still limps."

"I shouted at him to get out of the way, Zoë! I tried to brake, but it was too late."

"But you were going down *our* driveway in *our* car!"

"I know where I was, Zoë. One thing you always know is where you were when you were born, and where you were when you died." He leaned over and looked out the window. "I died right down the street by that oak tree." Then he socked his palm with his fist. "Pow!" he said. "What a crash! I never drove a car before!"

"I kept dreaming you came back, Maine, and now here you are!"

"Not for long," he said. "I came back on a Saturday morning when I knew your folks would be out, your brother over on Heartsunk skating, and you'd probably be here alone."

I shivered.

"Don't tremble. I'm not going to hurt you. I just want you to stop dreaming about me. Could you please put me out of your head altogether?"

"How did you know I—"

He cut me off. "We always know because we can't rest if people dream of us. It's been a year now, Zoë. When my family died, I stopped dreaming of them after about a week."

I didn't say the obvious: that he hadn't liked his family, but that I had been crazy about him.

He said, "I had no friends but you and Carl. He's *never* dreamed of me. But you do."

"Yes, I do. Not so much lately, but I definitely do."

"Don't!" Maine said. "I don't want to spend the rest of my time in eternity waiting for you to stop dreaming of me. I want to escape life forever . . . to sleep, finally!"

"It's just that I always felt so close to you, Maine."

"Don't be like my mother. She had this crush on a rock star

she'd never even talked to. After he died in a plane crash, she still kept obsessing about him, even after she got married."

I said, "Am I obsessing? I don't think of it *that* way."

He went right on. "Mother dreamed of him all the time. . . . Then when I was born, I was filled with his spirit. I was born a revenant. That's what made me so different."

"But you said you're a revenant *now*?"

"I was then and I am still. Only now I know what I am. After my encounter with that oak tree down the street I got back my eternal memory. Then I knew why I had never warmed to anyone. It's a revenant trait, you see: We don't warm to live people. Our hearts are so ancient and weary. We feel distanced."

"But you felt close to Carl and me."

"He was the only guy at school who could stand me. So I hung around here. But I didn't feel close to anyone. Not even your parents, and particularly not my parents."

I could feel my heart banging under my blouse, but my voice didn't give anything away. I said, "Did your mother know what you were?"

"Yes. She was warned just as I'm warning you. The rock star told her to let go, that if she didn't he'd return in one form or another, as a revenant."

"Your poor mother!"

Maine threw his head back and roared. "That's a good one! How about poor me? . . . Mommy thought it was fascinating. She even told my father. Anyone else would have thought she didn't have all her marbles, but *he* was fascinated, too. I was their little experiment. They became obsessed with the occult. That happens to people. They get a taste of the eternal and they do strange things: go to séances, hang out with others like them, buy Ouija boards, write creepy screenplays. . . . And they found out everything they could about revenants. They found out that we thrive in cold climates, that it's best to name us after a cold place. Best to stamp cold symbols somewhere on us: a pinecone, a snowbird, something like that. It's supposed to keep us calm."

I stared at his tattoo and felt a chill.

Maine said, "They followed all the rules in the beginning, but I wasn't much like her old rock star crush. Every revenant needs a spirit to ride back on, but the resemblance stops there. We go our own way, whether we're flesh or vapor." He shook his head, flashed me one of his lopsided smiles. "They just didn't like me. No one ever really does."

"I did," I said. "I still do."

"It's fading, though. You said so yourself. . . . And that's exactly why I'm here."

Then his blue eyes looked directly into mine. "Say this sentence with me, Zoë, okay?"

"Okay."

"I will not dream of Maine."

"I will not dream of Maine," I said.

"Say it over and over to yourself," he said. "Say good-bye forever."

"Good-bye forever."

I looked away because I didn't want him to see my tears.

When I looked again, Maine Foremann was gone.

The only thing I could find on revenants in our library was one paragraph in an occult book. It said the revenant spirit returns sometimes seen, sometimes unseen. Of all ghosts, revenants were the slickest and trickiest.

And I believed it. For what I could not accept was Maine's claim he did not feel *anything* for me. I told myself it was his way of keeping me from dreaming of him. The only way he could be free was to burst my bubble.

I wanted to be free of him, as well. It was time for me to grow up and get a life. I replaced my thick glasses with contact lenses, began studying *Vogue* when I was at the hairdresser's, even suffered through a performance of *The Sound of Music,* with Nelson Rider singing off-key.

Still . . . although it was fairly long since I had allowed myself to think of Maine for more than a pinch of time, often there was a shadow and a glimpse of a bare arm with a white tassel marked upon it, passing through my dreams.

One summer, Carl was home from college, and he brought a movie from the video store one night.

"Guess who made it?" he said, after dinner. "Maine Foremann's father."

"That poor crazy kid!" our father said. "May he rest in peace."

"Amen!" I said.

I didn't want to see *Born on Cold Nights.*

I went into the kitchen and stacked the dishes in the dishwasher. Carl would shout at me from time to time, "Zoë! Come in and watch this! This is weird, Zoë!"

"I'm going out."

"Again?" my father called in to me.

"Again," I said. "And I'm late. People are waiting for me."

"Zoë!" Carl wouldn't give up. "Hey, Zoë! Don't think of a yellow elephant!"

"What is that supposed to mean?" I peered around the corner at my brother.

"This guy playing the revenant says if you tell someone not to do something, they can't help doing it."

Just for a moment, I listened.

We are revenants with spirits that long to return as revenants. You humans with one life cannot know the joy of life again and again and yet again. Our desire is to return, and your dreaming makes it possible. But what if you stop dreaming of us? How can we prevent that?

My father shook his head. "Well, we did our best for the boy. But I have to admit that I don't miss him. Do you, Zoë?"

I just shrugged as though it wasn't a question that needed an answer.

Then I left the house, thinking of a yellow elephant, and hearing the low purr of a chuckle somewhere in the vapors of that summer evening.

I'VE GOT GLORIA

Hello? Mrs. Whitman?"

"Yes?"

"I've got Gloria."

"Oh, thank heaven! Is she all right?"

"She's fine, Mrs. Whitman."

"Where is she?"

"She's here with me."

"Who are you?"

"You can call me Bud."

"Bud who?"

"Never mind that, Mrs. Whitman. I've got your little dog and she's anxious to get back home."

"Oh, I know she is. She must miss me terribly. Where are you? I'll come and get her right away."

"Not so fast, Mrs. Whitman. First, there's a little something you must do."

"Anything. Just tell me where to find you."

"*I'll* find *you*, Mrs. Whitman, *after* you do as I say."

"What do you mean, Bud?"

"I mean that I'll need some money before I get Gloria home safely to you."

"Money?"

"She's a very valuable dog."

"Not really. I got her from the pound."

"But she's valuable to you, isn't she?"

"She's everything to me."

"So you have to prove it, Mrs. Whitman."

"What is this?"

"A dognapping. I have your dog and you have to pay to have her returned safely to you."

There was a pause.

I could just imagine her face—that face I hated ever since she flunked me. That mean, freckled face, with the glasses over those hard little green eyes, the small, pursed lips, the mop of frizzy red hair topping it all. . . . Well, top this, Mrs. Whitman: I do not even have that nutsy little bulldog of yours. She *is* lost, just as your countless signs nailed up everywhere announce that she is. . . . All I have is this one chance to get revenge, and I'm grabbing it!

Now her voice came carefully. "How much do you want?"

"A thousand dollars, Mrs. Whitman. A thou, in one-hundred-dollar bills, and Gloria will be back drooling on your lap."

"A *thousand* dollars?"

Got to you, didn't I? Did your stomach turn over the way mine did when I saw that F in math?

"Are you one of my students?"

"Oh, like I'm going to tell you if I am."

"You must be."

"I could be, couldn't I? You're not everyone's dream teacher, are you?"

"Please don't hurt my dog."

"I'm not cruel by nature."

I don't take after my old man. He said he was sorry that I flunked math because he knew how much I was counting on the hike through Yellowstone this summer. He said maybe the other guys would take some photographs so I could see what I was missing while I went to summer school to get a passing grade. "Gee, Scott," he said, "what a shame, and now you won't get an allowance, either, or have TV in your bedroom, or the use of the computer. But never mind, sonny boy," he said, "there'll be lots to do around the house. I'll leave lists for you every day of things to be done before I get home."

Mrs. Whitman whined, "I just don't have a thousand dollars. I don't know where I'll get so much money, either."

Sometimes I whined that way, and my mom would say, "Scotty, we wouldn't be so hard on you if you'd only take responsibility for your actions. We tell you to be in at eleven P.M. and you claim the bus was late. We ask you to take the tapes back to Videoland and you say we never said to do it. You always have an excuse for everything! You never blame yourself!"

"Mrs. Whitman? I don't mean to be hard on you but that's the deal, see. A thou in hundreds."

"Just don't hurt Gloria."

"Gee, what a shame that you have to worry about such a thing. She's a sweet little dog, and I know she misses you because she's not eating."

"She doesn't eat dog food, Bud. I cook for her."

"That's why she doesn't eat, hmm? I don't know how to cook."

"You could just put a frozen dinner in the microwave. A turkey dinner, or a Swanson's pot roast. I'll pay you for it."

"A thousand dollars plus ten for frozen dinners? Is that what you're suggesting?"

"Let me think. Please. I have to think how I can get the money."

"Of course you do. I'll call you back, Mrs. Whitman, and meanwhile I'll go to the store and get some Swanson's frozen dinners."

"When will you—"

I hung up.

I could hear Dad coming up the stairs.

"Scott?"

"Yes, sir?"

"I'm going to take the Saturn in for an oil change. I want you to come with me."

"I have some homework, sir."

"I want you to come with me. *Now*."

In the car, he said, "We need to talk."

"About what?" I said.

There was one of her Lost Dog signs tacked to the telephone pole at the end of our street.

"We need to talk about this summer," he said.

"What about it?"

"You *have* to make up the math grade. That you *have* to do. I'm sorry you can't go to Yellowstone."

"Yeah."

"There's no other way if you want to get into any kind of college. Your other grades are fine. But you need math. . . . What's so hard about math, Scott?"

"I hate it!"

"I did, too, but I learned it. You have to study."

"Mrs. Whitman doesn't like me."

"Why doesn't she like you?"

"She doesn't like anyone but that bulldog."

"Who's lost, apparently."

"Yeah."

"The signs are everywhere."

"Yeah."

"But she wouldn't deliberately flunk you, would she?"

"Who knows?"

"Do you really think a teacher would flunk you because she doesn't like you?"

"Who knows?"

"Scott, you've got to admit when you're wrong. I'll give you an example. I was wrong when I said you couldn't have an allowance or TV or use of the computer, etcetera. I was angry and I just blew! That was wrong. It wouldn't have made it any easier for you while you're trying to get a passing grade in math. So I was wrong! I apologize and I take it back."

"How come?"

"How come? Because I'm sorry. I thought about it and it bothered me. I'm a hothead, and I don't like that about myself. Okay?"

"Yeah."

"Maybe that's what's wrong here."

"What's wrong where?"

"Between us."

"Is something wrong between us?"

"Scotty, I'm trying to talk with you. About us. I want to work things out so we get along better."

"Yeah."

"Sometimes I do or say rash things."

"Yeah."

"I always feel lousy after."

"Oh, yeah?"

"Do you understand? I shouldn't take things out on you. That's petty. Life is hard enough. We don't have to be mean and spiteful with each other. Agreed?"

"Yeah." I was thinking about the time our dog didn't come home one night. I couldn't sleep. I even prayed. When he got back all muddy the next morning, I broke into tears and told him, "Now you're making me blubber like a baby!"

Dad was still on my case.

"Scott, I want you to think about why Mrs. Whitman flunked you."

"I just told you: she doesn't like me."

"Are you really convinced that you're good at math but the reason you failed was because she doesn't like you?"

"Maybe."

"Is she a good teacher?"

"She never smiles. She's got these tight little lips and these ugly freckles."

"So she's not a good teacher?"

"I can't learn from her."

"Did you study hard?"

"I studied. Sure. I studied."

"How many others flunked math?"

"What?"

"How many others flunked math?"

"No one."

"Speak up."

"I said, I'm the only one."

"So others learn from her despite her tight little lips and ugly freckles?"

"I guess."

"Scott, who's to blame for your flunking math?"

"Okay," I said. "Okay."

"Who is to blame?"

"Me. Okay? I didn't study that hard."

He sighed and said, "There. Good. You've accepted the blame. . . . How do you feel?"

"I feel okay." I really didn't, though. I was thinking about that dumb bulldog running loose somewhere, and about Mrs. Whitman worried sick now that she thought Gloria'd been dognapped.

Dad said, "I think we both feel a lot better."

We sat around in the waiting room at Saturn.

Dad read *Sports Illustrated,* but I couldn't concentrate on the magazines there or the ballgame on TV. I was down. I knew what Dad meant when he'd told me he felt bad after he "blew" and that he didn't like himself for it.

I kept glancing toward the pay phone. I stuck my hands in my pants pockets. I had a few quarters.

"I'm going to call Al and see what he's doing tonight," I said.

Dad said, "Wait until you get home. We'll be leaving here very shortly."

"I'm going to look around," I said.

I didn't know Mrs. Whitman's number. I'd copied it down from one of the Lost Dog signs and ripped it up after I'd called her. I hadn't planned to follow up the call, get money from her: nothing like that. I just wanted to give her a good scare.

I went over to the phone book and looked her up.

Then I ducked inside the phone booth, fed the slot a quarter, and dialed.

"Hello?"

"Mrs. Whitman? I don't have your dog. I was playing a joke."

"I know you don't have my dog. Gloria's home. The dog warden found her and brought her back right after you hung up on me."

I was relieved. At least she wouldn't have to go all night worrying about getting Gloria back.

"I was wrong," I said. "It was petty. I'm sorry."

"Do you know what you put me through, Scott Perkins?"

I just hung up.

I stood there with my face flaming.

"Scott?" My father was looking all over for me, calling me and calling me. "Scott! Are you here? The car's ready!"

All the way home he lectured me on how contrary I was. Why couldn't I have waited to phone Al? What was it about me that made me just go ahead and do something I was expressly told I shouldn't do? "Just when I think we've gotten someplace," he said, "you turn around and go against my wishes.

"*Why*?" he shouted.

I said, "What?" I hadn't been concentrating on all that he was saying. I was thinking that now she knew my name—don't ask me how—and now what was she going to do about it?

"I asked you *why* you go against my wishes," Dad said. "Nothing I say seems to register with you."

"It registers with me," I said. "I just seem to screw up sometimes."

"I can hardly believe my ears." He was smiling. "You actually said sometimes you screw up. That's a new one."

"Yeah," I said. "That's a new one."

Then we both laughed, but I was still shaking, remembering Mrs. Whitman saying my name that way.

When we got in the house, Mom said, "The funniest thing happened while you were gone. The phone rang and this woman asked what number this was. I told her, and she asked whom she was speaking to. I told her and she said, 'Perkins . . . Perkins. Do you have a boy named Scott?' I said that we did, and she said, 'This is Martha Whitman. Tell him I'll see him this summer. I'm teaching remedial math.'"

I figured that right after I'd hung up from calling her about Gloria, she'd dialed *69. I'd heard you could do that. The phone would ring whoever called you last. That was why she'd asked my mother what number it was and who was speaking.

Dad said, "You see, Scott, Mrs. Whitman doesn't dislike you, or she wouldn't have called here to tell you she'd see you this summer."

81

"I was wrong," I said. "Wrong again."
Oh, was I ever!

GRACE

Sunday mornings when my father stepped up to the pulpit, I could almost hear the congregation groaning inside, saying to themselves: *Here we go again, another of Yawn's boring sermons.*

The best thing about Reverend Edward Yourn was that he looked so earnest and impassioned. Sincere blue eyes, silky black hair, this fine smile—I hoped I'd keep looking like him, because he's great that way. If you hadn't heard him begin by announcing that his subject that morning was "Worship as a Time for Realignment," you might have thought he was going to kick off a really provocative meditation the way they say Father Garzarella does at Holy Family. The sermon board down there promised things like "I Don't Believe the Bible," and "Heeeeerrrrre's Jesus!"

Dad announced "Religion Without Righteousness," or "The Meaning of Redemption."

"Daddy has a more formal style," my mother claimed "Some people prefer that."

"Mom, his nickname is Yawn. In college they called him Snore."

"It's just a play on our last name, Teddy."

"I don't have nicknames like that. And I'm Ted, or Teddy Yourn. Dad is always Edward."

"Not always." Mom smiled. "I call him lots of things besides Edward."

I am not a religious person. Dad said that a good many Preachers' Kids, in their teens, were not religious people. P.K. have to grow into it, Dad said.

I was fifteen. "I don't think I ever will," I told him. "You *always* were. We're different."

"How do you know I always was?"

"The kids called you Preacher in your high school yearbook."

He'd get red whenever I mentioned the yearbook. He *was* probably afraid I was going to tease him about the infamous inscription from Taylor Train, known to us rock fans as Choo Choo or Chooch.

Dad went to school with him back in Columbia, Missouri.

When Chooch played concerts out in Montauk, about five miles from us on Long Island, the tickets were sold out months ahead of time. Locals would give up trying to get tickets, there were so many presolds, so many scalpers in on the action. And he literally stopped traffic. It was a good time to head for the beach.

When I was younger and stupid, I'd bring out Dad's yearbook to show kids. Who'd believe Dad not only went to school with Choo Choo but also was on the same page with him? That was before I knew that what I was really showing everyone was that my dad was a dork, world-class. The kids in his class wrote stuff like "Best wishes to The Preacher from Paul," or "Good luck, Edward, with your ambition to spread the good word! Marilyn!"

The only one who wrote anything beyond one polite sentence was Taylor Train. He drew a bubble over his own head with zzzzzs inside it, and made his eyelids look closed. Then he drew an arrow over to Dad's photograph and wrote *This is me listening to you preach someday in the future, Edward! I bet you convert the world to atheism! Why is it always losers who go after sinners? T. T. Train.*

"No one's asking you to be religious," Dad said. "Just have grace."

"Grace under pressure." I smirked, regretting it instantly, because I really wasn't out to get Dad. I loved him. But he'd put that Hemingway quote about grace up on the sermon board once, and someone had taken a magic marker and drawn underneath it this picture of a naked girl being stomped on by a grinning gorilla.

"Don't ever let any joker spoil the word *grace* for you, Teddy," Dad said. "I don't ask you to believe in anything you can't yet feel, but I do hope you'll have grace."

"That sounds a little dirty to me, Dad." Why was I always after him? Was it because he embarrassed me Sundays with those zzzzz sermons? Was I just self-conscious being a non-believing P.K.?

Dad said, "When you learn what grace is, it won't sound that way to you."

"I know what it is. It's doing the right thing."

Dad said, "It's doing the right thing and then more."

We left it at that.

When I was a little kid, I idolized Dad. I thought he was the best, and all I wanted to do was grow up and be like him.

Then little by little—a little more every year—it began to dawn on me that he wasn't this great knight in armor I'd made him out to be. He was far from it.

Even people in his own congregation thought he lacked charisma. Some of the younger members said the day would come when the old diehards would pass away. Then they'd junk Dad.

The way I learned about all this was the way kids in a small town hear the word about their parents. "My father says your father is . . ."

Not up-to-date. Not bringing in enough young people because he's behind the times. And the old familiar word: *boring.*

I remember a Sunday when we had a covered-dish dinner after church at the manse. It was over in a few hours. Meanwhile, Holy Family got bused down to the beach to dance and picnic, staying to watch the sunset. Even First Methodist thought up the idea of a sleigh ride one winter, going from house to house to pick up the parishioners and take them to the church hall for a square dance. Rabbi Silver, a big movie fan, instituted Flick Night on the synagogue grounds, Thursdays.

You couldn't fault Dad when it came to helping families get through illnesses or hard financial times—he was always right there in a pinch, but folks said he was better at sympathizing than socializing.

Mom was a little that way herself. She was better at repairing broken dolls and dressing them up for the Christmas boxes, and baking things for our churchyard Books and Cookies sales . . . but her idea of a Saturday night was reading a book, while Dad (always a last-minute writer) worked on his sermon. Sometimes the three of us watched an old film, or played Scrabble.

In church I went through the motions, and I suffered through the sermons. (*Good Lord, Dad, don't tempt Fate with a sermon on "How We Silence the Bible." You raise the question "But How Do We Silence the Minister?"*) I became an okay athlete (soccer, tennis, wrestling), and I was in all the school plays. I grew to look like Dad, so I was fairly popular.

Then in my senior year I fell in love with a Korean girl named Jenifer Koh.

Because of her, that last year of high school was perfect. Both of us had jobs at the Gap after school. Both of us thought about skipping college, going right to New York, where I'd try out for theater and Jenifer would get a job in fashion. Both of us were into the same things: same music, same books and movies, same way of hanging out. We just plain enjoyed each other.

The only thing we didn't agree on was the postgraduation dinner party at Springside Inn. I wanted to skip it. We were going to the prom two weeks before the ceremony, and that was enough celebration from my point of view. But Jenny said she'd feel let down if we didn't have someplace to go after we were in our caps and gowns, particularly if the other seniors had plans.

Not all the other seniors *did* have plans. The party at Springside was going to cost a lot. A special jitney would take us up there, and a photographer would be tailing us to make sure we'd have a permanent record of the evening. Long Island T was playing for dancing afterward. It would come to $300 a couple.

Dad wanted me to take our names off the list.

"You don't have to pay for it." I said. "I have savings." He was already shelling out for the prom.

"That isn't why I don't want you to go, Ted. I've heard that some of your classmates feel left out. It's one thing to splurge for your high school prom—okay—but it's something else when right on top of it there's this special party for the elite after the graduation ceremony. I don't like it."

"What does that mean, that I can't go?"

"It means I wish you'd reconsider."

"Jenny really wants to do it. Dad. All our crowd is going!"

"Maybe when I tell her what *I* have planned, she'll change her mind."

"Oh, Dad." I couldn't imagine what he thought he could come up with that would make anyone change their minds, much less Jenifer.

"Well, Teddy, I've made some calls and word is out. I'm opening the Meeting House hall for a party after the ceremony. Fortunately, people can just walk here from school."

I groaned again. "Dad, no one wants to come to the First Presbyterian Meeting House to celebrate!"

"Free of charge."

"Dad, you couldn't *pay* kids to do it!"

"I think you're wrong about that, Son."

"Don't do this to yourself, Dad."

"It's already done. Taylor is coming by about eight o'clock. Everyone will have eaten by then. We'll have our ladies prepare their roast chicken and mashed with—"

"Wait a minute. . . . Wait. Taylor?"

"I think you call him Chooch."

"Choo Choo Taylor is coming here?"

"He has a concert the very next night in Montauk. He said he thought it would be fun."

Mom piped up. "He said, 'Hey, Preacher Man, that sounds like it'd be a ball!' I was on the extension."

Mom was all smiles, her face aglow, and Dad looked pretty pleased with himself. He said, "We're not going to tell the newspapers ahead of time."

"We know all the names of the kids who aren't on the Springside list, and we're quietly calling them," Mom said.

"Are you telling them Chooch is going to show up?"

"Of course," said Mom. "We're asking them to try and keep it to themselves. We just don't want gate-crashers."

I kept looking from one to the other, unable to believe my ears. "Dad, did you just call him up out of the blue? Did he remember you?"

"Oh, he remembered your father, honey. We told the concert manager that Reverend Yourn had to get in touch with Chooch, and before we knew it, he called back. He said, 'How long has it been, Edward?' I was on the extension!"

"I can't believe you had the nerve!" I told Dad.

"He had the nerve," Mom said, "because he wasn't doing it for himself."

"Oh, I'll be glad to see Taylor again," said Dad.

Jenifer couldn't believe it, either. I'd never even told her about Dad going to school with him, because I didn't want to drag out the yearbook to prove it . . . and then have her see the zzzzzz's.

Jenifer liked Dad. She said he was a little like her own father: reserved.

"My grandfather was a preacher too," I told her. "He was reserved too."

"Of course we're going to cancel Springside," Jenifer said. "Choo Choo Train!" Jenifer said. . . . Jenifer said, "I can't believe it, Teddy!"

In school those last weeks I'd suddenly see a sly grin on the face of little Buddy Tonsetter, whose backpack always seemed bigger than he was, or a wink from Ellie Tutton, who was a foster child in this big family that specialized in kids of all colors and races. I felt a nudge in the hall from Karl Renner, whose dad had died of heart failure at Easter; and Dana Klaich, who worked at the Gap with Jenny and me, gave me a two-fingered salute in Cafeteria.

There were some cynical looks, too, from the wiseacres who hung out and mocked every tradition, ceremony, holiday—whatever; they were above it. Cal, Peter, Leary, Judge. But they weren't above Chooch. One of them would call out something like "We'll be seeing you, Yourn," in this singsong threatening way, as though they were saying: Your old man better produce, kiddo!

I was getting nervous, then more nervous, then terrified.

Holy Cow, I thought, *this is going to be some big mess if Chooch doesn't show . . . and why should he show? He didn't even like my father. Why should he show?*

That was like a chant in my head: *Whyshouldheshow? Whyshouldheshow?* The night before graduation I actually prayed. I don't pray often, because I don't think there's anyone really there to hear me, but *I* could hear me, and it was reassuring to me that I'd go to any lengths not to have this turn out the way I was ninety percent sure it would.

All through graduation that was what I thought about. At least someday I'd be able to tell my kids what was on my mind back then. How many parents can claim to remember that?

I prayed: *Please let him come. Please don't let this be a disaster.* I thought: *Is this praying or thinking?* I thought: *Is this wishing or dreading?*

I thought: *Oh shut up, Teddy! What will be will be!*

And then . . . then there we all were in the Meeting House, seated at four round tables decorated with roses from our garden, a few white balloons floating overhead . . . and Mom had even gone through my CDs to find Chooch's music. It was right up front with Mick Jagger, Billy Joel—all the ones who'd been around forever and would last that long, too. They were the ones at the heart of rock 'n' roll, the kind of performers who could make kids go ape.

Chooch's voice was rocking through the speakers.

The church ladies had cooked up a storm, and everybody was scarfing it down, talking, laughing, having a good time. But everybody was looking toward the door, too—in high gear, waiting, watching the clock.

Then it began. "Choo Choo Choo Choo"—kids imitating a train the way they did at his concerts when he'd walk onstage with his guitar strapped to him. "Choochoochoochoochoo!"

He had come in the back way.

He was slapping the backs of the boys at the first table, and blowing kisses at the girls, and they had started the *choo*-ing. Now the whole place was making that noise, and kids were on their feet, clapping, with Chooch heading toward my father's table, where there was a mike.

My father stood up, and Chooch gave him a sock on the shoulder, then leaned down and shook hands with my mother. "Shut up now!" he said over the mike. "I'm going to sing for my supper. I'm going to sing two songs now and then I'm going to eat. Then I'm going to sing two songs more, and I'm out of here!"

He sang his big hit, "I Came Back to Say Good-bye," and next he sang "Heartless Woman."

Jenifer and I were at Dad's table, and I was trying to get Dad's eye, trying to tell him some way, *Hey, Pop, you pulled it off! You did it!* But Dad was watching him, nodding a little to the music, a smile at the corners of his lips.

When Chooch was through with the two songs, he said over the applause. "Let me eat in peace now, or no more music!"

The church ladies came hurrying out of the kitchen with hot chicken and mashed for him, and biscuits and gravy, and most of us helped ourselves to seconds to keep Chooch company.

"This is my son, Ted," my father said.

Chooch said, "Chip off the old block?"

My father nodded.

Then Chooch said to me, "Lord, I hope not! I hope you're not the stuffed shirt your old man was in high school."

I saw Dad's eyes blink while I tried to think of an answer to that.

Under her breath, Jenifer said, "That's not nice."

Chooch wolfed down the chicken, mouth open while he chewed, and told everybody, "I couldn't believe Pastor Snore was on the horn to me. I told my manager: This I gotta see! This guy was a dead head in school, and I don't mean he followed around after the Grateful Dead. He was a dead head." Chooch let his head drop on his shoulder, acting out what he was saying.

The kids were laughing.

"Of course, Edward, here—we always called him Edward. He was no Eddie, were you, Edward? Edward here probably never expected I'd turn up at his place for any reason other than to ask for a loan, or ask him to hide me from the law or something nefarious. How do you like that word—*nefarious*? You like it, Edward?"

"It's a good word," my father said quietly.

"It's the way you think of me, probably. I haven't changed, either, if that's what you thought. There's no God in my blanking life, and thank you, Taylor Train, for saying 'blanking.' When we all know what I *really* mean."

The kids at our table were exchanging puzzled looks.

My mother said, "We really appreciate your coming out of your way to do this for us."

"So you're the gal who married Snore?" Chooch said.

"I'm happy to say I am," said my mother.

"Happy to say she is," said Chooch, and then he dropped his head to his shoulder and made a snoring sound.

By the time he got up to do two more songs, Jenifer was whispering that he was a pig, not worthy of sitting at my father's feet, much less at his table.

There were four kids sitting there who'd heard Chooch. He'd

barely taken a breath between insults aimed at Dad. The kids had grown quiet, and their smiles had faded as they began to realize that for some reason Chooch was bent on humiliating Dad. Mom was looking down at her lap, mostly, and Dad was looking straight ahead.

Everybody else in the place was up on their feet, arms in the air, hands fisted, crying out happily, "Whoa! Whoa!" at the end of each number, whistling, squealing. They had gotten what they'd come for.

I'll never know what made Chooch do four more numbers than he'd announced, or what made him take questions and sign autographs. I'll never know why he agreed to come at all.

Mom thought perhaps it was an attempt to soften his image, since he had seen to it that the next day newspapers would report his good deed.

Dad said that maybe he identified with the kids: the ones who couldn't afford the big dinner dance, the ones who weren't coupled, the loners, the cynics, the outsiders. You should have seen their faces that night. You should have seen Cal, Peter, Leary, and Judge!

Chooch even tossed Ellie Tutton his cap . . . which took guts because his hair was thinning.

All the kids were following him out the door except the ones at our table.

"He was mean to you, Reverend," Billy Tonsetter said.

"He makes jokes, Billy."

"He's not *all* bad," Mom said.

"I don't like him anymore, though," said Jenifer. "He's not respectful."

"No, he's not," Dad said. "But he kept his word."

. . .

I thought about that evening forever.

I'll think forever about that evening.

My father must have known that anyone who wrote that in his yearbook, who had become a nefarious (thanks, Chooch) rock singer not known for his gentle demeanor, could probably not be counted on to behave politely toward a man of the cloth he'd never taken to when he was a boy.

My father must have known what he'd be up against with Chooch, as surely as he'd known the only way to rescue the outsiders after the graduation ceremony was to get Chooch there . . . somehow.

And Dad did.

Choo Choo Train kept his word . . . and then more.

And my father, in my eyes that evening, became my hero again . . . and then more.

I'm the same unbeliever that I was before I went off to New York, but I know what grace is now . . . and I try for that.

I try to be like Dad.

GUESS WHO'S
BACK IN TOWN, DEAR?

Prom night. After Drew got sick, he sat in his new white sports car with the door open. He sat where he'd never sat, and would likely never sit again: opposite the driver's seat.

"Are you okay now?" Tory asked him.

Drew couldn't answer her right away. He was holding his head up with one hand, his hair falling over his face. He was blond and green-eyed like Tory. People said they looked enough alike to be brother and sister.

She had never seen Drew drunk. She knew he'd gone into the boys' john with some of the seniors so he wouldn't come across as a stuck-up preppie, too good for his old crowd.

"I have to go home, Tor. I'm really sorry."

"That's all right."

"No, it is not all right, and I'm sorry."

She waited to see if he'd get behind the wheel. She wondered if he remembered that she didn't know how to operate a stick shift.

She stood there in her new long white gown. There was no way she could go to the after-prom party alone, even though Drew had paid the hundred-dollar-a-couple charge for the band and breakfast. No one went alone.

The highlight of the prom was the Elvis impersonator. Tory could hear him from the parking lot. He was singing "It's Now or Never." He was good, too.

Drew was holding his face with both hands.

Tory looked down at the red carnation that had fallen to the gravel from his lapel. She thought of painting what she saw and calling it "Prom Night." She picked up the flower and held it.

"Do you need some help, Miss Victoria King?"

He was the one who'd worn a pink dinner jacket to the dance. Drew had nicknamed him "The Flamingo." His real name had been forgotten by most everyone, since he'd come to school in the middle of senior year.

He had black curly hair and brown eyes, was medium height and on the skinny side.

Tory said, "I don't think we've really met, have we?"

"My mother works for your mother."

"You mean Maria?" She was the Kings' new maid.

He nodded. "I'm Horacio Vargas. How can I help here?"

Luckily, he'd come to the prom stag.

He drove Tory home first.

He was from New York City, he said, and someday he was going to write a novel. But first he would become a lawyer. He already knew a lot about law, and he read all the time.

When he asked her what she was planning to do, she said she was going to Vassar, and so was Drew.

"To become what?"

"College graduates," she laughed. But when he didn't seem to think her answer was all that funny, she said, "Drew will go into real estate with my dad. He'll buy houses, and I'll fix them up to sell . . . maybe."

"Maybe?"

"We'll see. . . . We're coming back here to live."

"You sounded like there was more. You said 'maybe' as if you had a secret wish."

"We'll come back and live up on the lake. We both love the lake."

Drew was curled up in a fetal position in the small space behind them.

"This city gives me the shivers, though," said Horacio.

"Because of the prison?" Arcade was known for that.

"There it is to remind you how you can go so wrong."

Horacio hitchhiked home that night after he helped Drew's father carry him inside.

He put the carnation she'd given him inside his Bible.

After he told his mother what had happened, he added, "If I had such a girl for my date, I wouldn't be passing the bottle in the boys' toilet."

"Victoria King ruined your prom night," his mom said. "You didn't rent that beautiful jacket to be a chauffeur!"

"What about her night?"

"Worry about yourself, Horacio, not them. They won't ever worry about you, you can count on that."

Mr. Victor King, a prominent Arcade realtor, enjoys telling the following about a certain New Year's Eve in New York City.

Invited there by a client, he and Mrs. King were not

unpleasantly surprised when it was explained that after dinner everyone was heading in limos to Grand Central Station, to hand out sandwiches to the homeless.

Mrs. King was secretly apprehensive that one of them might call her names or indulge in threatening behavior.

"Not to worry, Mrs. Best Friend," Mr. King reassured, using his pet name for her. "The mayor himself is going to be there. You'll be well protected."

Mr. King borrowed an old baseball cap from his host and put on his Nike running clothes, which he took everywhere with him since his cholesterol had gone over 300.

At Grand Central, he set off to hand out salami heroes in the tunnels around the subways, while Mrs. King joined the ladies at the tables in the main waiting room.

The thing is—on Victor King's way back, as he was walking along by himself, someone tried to give *him* a sandwich!

Victor King always cracks up telling the story, and when he gets control again, he says, "I had to tell the fellow, thanks, but *I'm* one of *you!*"

"Thanks for the other night," Tory said.

She'd gone purposely to the A & P to find him, after Maria'd told her that was where he worked.

Drew parked outside, waiting for her, another couple in the back of his car. They were all old friends who'd been sailing their Stars and Comets alongside one another and swimming at the club together since they were little.

Drew had given Tory an envelope with a fifty-dollar bill inside.

"Is this money?" Horacio said, not waiting for an answer. He shook his head and handed back the envelope.

"It's not from me, Horatio. It's from Drew."

He had on a long white apron, and he was carrying a mop. He was cleaning up after someone who'd dropped a jar of pickles on the cement floor.

"But how can I ever return the favor?" Tory asked him. "It's not fair to make me indebted to you, Horacio."

His shirtsleeves were rolled. There was a silver identification bracelet clanking against his Timex.

Drew never wore jewelry, not even a class ring.

Neither did Tory's father.

Both of them agreed rings were not right for men, not even wedding rings.

"I like books," Horacio said. "You can buy me a paperback. You can buy me any paperback by Gabriel García Márquez."

Tory wrote down the name, since she had never heard of that author.

"A gift for the maid's boy?" Mrs. King said, amazed.

"I told you about it. You never listen."

"I listen. It's a little extreme, darling. Do you know why Maria moved to Arcade?"

"I suppose you're going to say she's some prisoner's relative."

"I'm afraid I am. . . . Her husband is in Arcade Prison."

Tory remembered her father's harangues about the "riffraff" moving right into Arcade, instead of just visiting their jailbird relatives. Mr. King often said he didn't mind paying taxes for schools and roads and hospitals, but he *did* mind shelling out for welfare for the "junkies' families."

"Those are junkies inside those walls. They're not like our old convicts," he'd say, as though he had fond memories of thieves and murderers from bygone days.

"Maria works hard," Mrs. King told Tory while Tory tied a red ribbon around the package for Horacio. "But her husband got in there because of drugs, so I thought I'd just not mention anything. You know how your father hates addicts."

"What about some of his friends up at the country club? You could pour them out of there weekends."

"Oh, that's apples and oranges you're trying to compare, Tory. Why, you even drew one of your little sketches on the wrapping paper, and is that a note you're enclosing?"

"It's just a thank-you note, Mother . . . and yes, I did one of my little sketches on the paper." Tory hated that certain condescending tone her mother would get at times.

This is the note Tory'd written to Horacio:

I read a little of this and I love it, so I bought a copy for myself too.
Thanks for telling me about this author, Horacio.
Next time I see you we can discuss Love in the Time of Cholera. *I do*
have a secret wish. It is to be a painter.

She'd signed her name *Victoria*, though no one called her that except for him, that first time on prom night.

Another story Mr. King enjoys telling always begins with the time he called upstairs to his wife, "Laura? Guess who's back in town, dear?"

He often retells it when they're out dining with their special crowd, all long-time Arcadians, all with clear memories of Richard Lasher.

Only teachers called him by his first name.

He was a troublemaker from the start, so good-looking more than one Arcadian said some talent scout ought to see him. Let Hollywood deal with Lasher!

Mrs. King thought he was like some wild and beautiful weed appearing suddenly on a grand green lawn.

He'd come to Arcade because of the prison, too.

But he'd come as the new warden's son.

Everyone said it was a good thing he knew his way around the prison. He'd have no trouble finding things when he got sent there.

One time he was picked up for shoplifting in the A & P and another time he drove off in someone's car on County Fair Day. He'd crawl into the Schine Cinema window from the fire escape, or he'd break into the YMCA after midnight for a skinny dip. He set a pig loose down a church aisle on a Sunday and he stole the iron balls from the Civil War memorial cannon on the village green.

Then when he grew up, it was girls. It was fathers keeping guard over their daughters, for fear he'd break one of their hearts or worse. Mostly it was "or worse" they worried about when it came to Lasher.

He was charming, devilish, a looker, and he had his own car. A van.

A *big* van, decorated hippy style, stereo inside and heaven knows what else.

And then . . . and everyone in Arcade remembered it—it was Lasher and Laura Waite.

"Before my time," Mr. King likes to say, with that cocky smile of his.

Mrs. King gets red, always. It is a story she doesn't think he should tell, not because she cares that Lasher has become a prison guard in Florida and a Born-Again. "Bald now, and *fat*? He breaks chairs. Swear it!" Mr. King often has to stop laughing before he can continue. "I didn't know who he was, he's so bloated."

For Mrs. King this particular story is not about what Lasher has become, as much as it is about what passion does to love when passion has a say in it.

Who didn't know what was going on between them? Who'd never seen the two of them together, how they couldn't keep their hands off each other, couldn't stop grinning and looking into each other's eyes?

Victor King continues: "Says, 'How's my Laura?' to me. *His* Laura!" Mr. King slaps his knee.

No, it is not what Lasher turned out to be that makes Mrs. King embarrassed for her husband.

No one can take back the fact that Laura Waite *was* Lasher's girl. Mrs. King thinks of it as ages and ages ago, the year she wrote the poem.

Her mother found it at the back of Laura's diary and demanded an explanation.

Laura said, "Why don't *you* explain why you snooped?"

"*Lips your lips on mine,*" her mother read sourly, "*And wet your eyes, eyes, eyes,/Not yet, not yet.* What does that mean?"

But Mrs. Waite knew the answer to that question. That

fall Laura found herself attending Miss Grey's for Girls, off in Pennsylvania.

In all her life she'd only written the one poem.

"What did you like about it?" Horacio asked.

Tory'd been passing by, somehow, just as the supermarket was closing for the night.

"That the hero was so intense, I think," said Tory. "And that it was really much more than just a love story."

"You know the author, García Márquez? I was born in the town where he was born. Aracataca, Colombia."

He took her hand then, just like that. Of course, they had come to a crossing, but he was going to hold it after they got to the other side. She knew it.

He said, "All that intensity is my birthright." He looked at her to test how her eyes would take that and he saw them shining back. Now he was almost sure of what he'd dared to hope when he first saw her lingering outside.

A night of firecrackers and stars.

They sat in the canvas chairs along the front lawn of the club, facing the lake. Drew had on white pants and a red T-shirt, long and lean in this, the last summer of their youth.

Tory had called it that a moment ago, holding a sparkler away from her yellow halter dress. Drew stretched his legs out in front of him and said that he expected his youth to last until the end of college.

"But it's the last time we'll be living with our parents, full-time. Did you ever think of that?"

"This will always be home," Drew said. "Did I tell you what

dad's giving us for a wedding present? Four of the ten acres he owns up on the lake. Neat, huh?"

"That's four years away," Tory said.

The Fourth of July was at full pitch, loud and spectacular in the sky above them.

"Dad's not developing his six acres, either. He and Mother will build on three and save three for the grandkids. We'll have our own compound."

"Do you love me, Drew?"

"No," he said, "I'm marrying you out of habit."

"That's not funny."

"Of course I love you. Who do I love if I don't love you?"

"Who do I love," she said, "if I don't love you?"

"Exactly," he said.

"No, not exactly." She started to tell him. . . . She was going to begin by asking him if he was ever curious what she did those evenings he spent watching sports on TV or going to ball games.

She tried to think of another way to start off, a way that would not put him on the defensive. Nothing he had done had anything to do with Horacio.

She was almost ready to do it, but in the pause he said, "That land's worth about thirty thousand an acre. In four more years, it'll be worth a lot more. We've really got it made, Tory!"

Rockets burst overhead and behind them the band began to play "Oh, Susannah."

One day a white rose was waiting for Tory when she came back from the club.

So was her mother.

"I'm sorry," Mrs. King said, "but the card fell out of the tissue paper, and I read it."

The card said, *The last line of LITOC from your H.*

LITOC stood for the novel by García Márquez.

"Well?" said Mrs. King. "What does it mean?"

"I'll have to look it up," said Tory, who'd never have to look it up to remember it.

"You know what I'm asking you. What is this all about, dear? He calls himself '*Your* H.'?"

"When you were in love with that Lasher, what was it all about?" Tory asked.

"Tory, Richard Lasher was the son of the warden. He wasn't the son of someone inside. He was of our own kind, not an ethnic. He went to middle school and high school here, and we all knew the family."

"I didn't ask you what Lasher was about. I asked you what *it* was about."

Mrs. King drew a deep breath.

She sat down on her daughter's bed.

She said finally, "When did all this happen?"

"If you get her in trouble, your life will be ruined," said Maria Vegas.

"I don't touch her."

"Sure, and I'm that blonde Madonna from the MTV."

"I don't. We're going away, Mama."

"What does your father say?"

"To go. To marry her."

"He said that?"

"He said when he fell in love and married it was the best thing of his life."

His mother blushed and bit away a little smile. "There's more to come," she said. "It's not over, tell him."

"And he thanked me for bringing her there to meet him, for asking him his opinion."

"What did he think, you'd leave your own father out?"

While she waits for him to come home this night, Mrs. King is thinking of things she has gone over and over in her head all day.

She thinks of the greeting card he always presents to her three times a year: on Valentine's Day, on their anniversary, and on her birthday. She finds one propped up against the water glass at her place, at the breakfast table. He is already at work by then, since they never eat together in the morning, and she immediately thanks him, telephoning his office to do so.

The cards are the big, mushy sort with words on them he would never dream of speaking.

She thinks, too, of his habit of telling her he feels like scratching an itch. It has become his way of saying that he's what Tory would call horny. Mrs. King hates that word, as well. Mrs. King thinks of it as wanting to make love, though that is not the most accurate description of what actually happens.

And Mrs. King remembers how surprised she used to be when she was with her girlfriends and they would admit to similar things going on in their lives. All of them did; all admitted it and laughed.

There was a warm camaraderie in the laughter, as though they all belonged to the same sorority . . . and one of them might say with a certain affectionate indignation, "Men!"

When she hears his car drive up, she steels herself. She tries to remember what Tory said to tell him: Vassar isn't the only college—New York City has several very fine ones, including Parsons School of Design, and Cooper Union, for artists. Tory does not expect any help from home, either. Both she and Horacio are going to find jobs in New York.

And Mrs. King is to try and make him understand that since Horacio came into her life, Tory realizes she did not love Drew that way at all. She was never in love with him. Drew was more like a best friend. No . . . Mrs. King decides to omit that description of Drew.

Wham!—the slam of the Chrysler's door, and now he is on his way up the walk.

Mrs. King's heart is racing with an excitement she has not felt for ages and ages.

They had composed their own marriage vows.

They were very simple ones, ending with Tory saying, "We, Victoria and Horacio, will love each other forever."

A pause for the exchange of rings.

Then it was Horacio's turn. "'Forever, he said,'" which is the last line of *Love in the Time of Cholera.*

THE GREEN KILLER

Be nice to him," my father said. "He's your cousin, after all."

"He takes my things."

"Don't be silly, Alan. What of yours could Blaze possibly want? He has everything . . . *everything,*" my father added with a slight tone of disdain, for we all knew how spoiled my cousin was.

But he did take my things. Not things he wanted because he needed them, but little things like a seashell I'd saved and polished, an Indian head nickel I'd found, a lucky stone shaped like a star. Every time he came from New York City with his family for a visit, some little thing of mine was missing after they left.

We were expecting them for Thanksgiving that year. It was our turn to do the holiday dinner with all our relatives. Everyone would be crowded into our dining room with extra card tables brought up from the cellar, and all sorts of things borrowed from the next-door neighbors: folding chairs, extra serving platters, one of those giant coffee pots that could serve twenty . . . on and on.

It was better when it was their turn and everyone trooped into New York for a gala feast in their Fifth Avenue apartment overlooking Central Park. They had a doorman to welcome us, a cook to make the turkey dinner, maids to serve us.

Blaze's father was the CEO of Dunn Industry. My father was the principal of Middle Grove High School on Long Island. About the only thing the two brothers had in common was a son apiece: brilliant, dazzling Blaze Dunn, seventeen; and yours truly, Alan Dunn, sixteen, average.

But that was a Thanksgiving no one in the family would ever get to enjoy or forget. An accident on the Long Island Expressway caused the cherry black Mercedes to overturn, and my cousin Blaze was killed instantly.

I had mixed emotions the day months later when I was invited into New York to take what I wanted of Blaze's things.

Did I want to wear those cashmere sweaters and wool jackets and pants I'd always envied, with their Ralph Lauren and Calvin Klein labels? The shoes—even the shoes fit me, British-made Brooks Brothers Church's. Suits from Paul Stuart. Even the torn jeans and salty denim jackets had a hyperelegant "preppy" tone.

Yes!

Yes, I wanted to have them! It would make up for all the times my stomach had turned over with envy when he walked into a room, and the niggling awareness always there that my cousin flaunted his riches before me with glee. And all the rest—his good looks (Blaze was almost beautiful with his tanned perfect face, long eyelashes, green eyes, shiny black hair); and of course he was a straight-A student. He was at ease in any social situation. More than at ease. He was an entertainer, a teller of stories, a boy who could make you listen and laugh.

Golden. He was a golden boy. My own mother admitted it. Special, unique, a winner—all of those things I'd heard said about Blaze. Even the name, never mind it was his mother's maiden name. Blaze Dunn. I used to imagine one day I'd see it up on the marquee of some Broadway theater, or on a book cover, or at the bottom of a painting in the Museum of Modern Art. He'd wanted to be an actor, a writer, a painter. His only problem, he had always said, was deciding which talent to stress.

While I packed up garment bags full of his clothes, I pictured him leering down from that up above where we imagine the dead watching us. I thought of him smirking at the sight of me there in his room, imagined him saying, "It's the only way *you'd* ever luck out like this, Snail!" He used to call me that. Snail. It was because I'd take naps when he was visiting. I couldn't help it. I'd get exhausted by him. I'd curl up in my room and hope he'd be gone when I'd wake up. . . . He said snails slept a lot, too. He'd won a prize once for an essay he'd written about snails. He'd described how snails left a sticky discharge under them as they moved, and he claimed that because of it a snail could crawl along the edge of a razor without cutting itself. . . . He'd have the whole dining table enthralled while he repeated things like that from his prize-winning essays. And while I retreated to my room to sleep— that was when he took my things.

All right. He took my things; I took *his* things.

I thought I might feel weird wearing his clothes, and even my mother wondered if I'd be comfortable in them. It was my father who thundered, "Ridiculous! Take advantage of your advantages! It's an inheritance, of sorts. You don't turn down *money* that's left you!"

Not only did I not feel all that weird in Blaze's clothes, I began to take on a new confidence. I think I even walked with a new, sure step. I know I became more outgoing, you might even say more popular. Not dazzling, no, not able to hold a room spellbound while I tossed out some information about the habits of insects, but in my own little high-school world out on Long Island I wasn't the old average Alan Dunn plodding along anymore. That spring I got elected to the prom committee, which decides the theme for the big end-of-the-year dance, and I even found the courage to ask Courtney Sweet out.

The only magic denied me by my inheritance seemed to be whatever it would take to propel me from being an average student with grades slipping down too often into Cs and Ds, up into Blaze's A and A-plus status. My newfound confidence had swept me into a social whirl that was affecting my studies. I was almost flunking science.

When I finally unpacked a few boxes of books and trivia that Blaze's mother had set aside for me, I found my seashell, my Indian head nickel, and my lucky stone. . . . And other things: a thin gold girl's bracelet, a silver key ring from Tiffany, initials H. J. K. A school ring of some sort with a ruby stone. A medal with two golf clubs crossed on its face. A lot of little things like that . . . and then a small red leather notebook the size of a playing card.

In very tiny writing inside, Blaze had listed initials, dates, and objects this way:

A.D.	December 25	Shell
H.K.	March 5	Key ring
A.D.	November 28	Indian nickel

He had filled several pages.

Obviously, I had not been the only one whose things Blaze had swiped. It was nothing personal.

As I flipped the pages, I saw more tiny writing in the back of the notebook.

A sentence saying: *"Everything is sweetened by risk."*

Another: *"Old burglars never die, they just steal away. (Ha! Ha!)"*

And: *"I dare, you don't. I have, you won't."*

Even today I wonder why I never told anyone about this. It was not because I wanted to protect Blaze or to leave the glorified memories of him undisturbed. I suppose it comes down to what I found at the bottom of one of the boxes.

The snail essay was there, and there was a paper written entirely in French. There was a composition describing a summer he had spent on the Cape, probably one of those "What I Did Last Summer" assignments unimaginative teachers give at the beginning of fall terms. . . . I did not bother to read beyond the opening sentences, which were "The Cape has always bored me to death for everyone goes there to have fun, clones with their golf clubs, tennis rackets, and volleyballs! There are no surprises on the Cape, no mysteries, no danger."

None of it interested me until I found "The Green Killer." It was an essay with an A-plus marked on it, and handwriting saying, "As usual, Blaze, you excel!"

The title made it sound like a Stephen King fantasy, but the essay was a description of an ordinary praying mantis . . . a neat and gory picture of the sharp spikes on his long legs that shot out, dug into an insect, and snap went his head!

"You think it is praying," Blaze had written, *"but it is waiting to kill!"*

My heart began pounding as I read, not because of any blood-thirsty instinct in me, but because an essay for science was due, and here was *my* chance to excel!

Blaze had gone to a private school in New York that demanded students handwrite their essays, so I carefully copied the essay into my computer, making a little bargain with Blaze's ghost as I printed it out: *I will not tell on you in return for borrowing your handiwork. Fair is fair. Your golden reputation will stay untarnished, while my sad showing in science will be enhanced through you.*

"The Green Killer" was an enormous hit! Mr. Van Fleet, our teacher, read it aloud, while I sat there beaming in Blaze's torn Polo jeans and light blue cashmere sweater. Nothing of mine had ever been read in class before. I had never received an A.

After class, Mr. Van Fleet informed me that he was entering the essay in a statewide science contest, and he congratulated me, adding, "You've changed, Alan. I don't mean just this essay—but *you.* Your personality. We've all noticed it." Then he gave me a friendly punch, and grinned slyly. "Maybe Courtney Sweet has inspired you.

And she was waiting for me by my locker, looking all over my face as she smiled at me, purring her congratulations.

Ah, Blaze, I thought, *finally, my dear cousin, you're my boy . . . and your secret is safe with me. That's our deal.*

•   •   •

Shortly after my essay was sent off to the science competition, Mr. Van Fleet asked me to stay after class again.

"Everyone," he said, "was impressed with 'The Green Killer,' Alan. Everyone agreed it was remarkable."

"Thank you," I said, unbuttoning my Ralph Lauren blazer, breathing a sigh of pleasure, rocking back and forth in my Church's loafers.

"And why not?" Mr. Van Fleet continued. "It was copied word for word from an essay written by Isaac Asimov. One of the judges spotted it immediately."

So Blaze was Blaze—even dead he'd managed to take something from me once again.

GREAT EXPECTATIONS

Hello, son."

"Hi there!" I don't think he noticed that I'd stopped calling him Dad. Not just because he wasn't my dad, but because I wished with all my heart he was. I wished I'd never become involved in this masquerade, and yet if I hadn't, I never would have *met* Onondaga John.

It was a warm, early spring day, surprising in upstate New York, where we often have snow up to our downstairs windows in March.

We sat in the prison visiting room. This was our third meeting. The first had been at Thanksgiving. The second at Christmas.

John Klee's face was lit by the few bars of sun that came through the high windows in the place. He had deep blue eyes, the color of his uniform. He told me once there was a saying: *True blue will never stain.* It meant that a truly noble heart will never disgrace itself . . . but it also referred to the blue aprons worn by butchers, which wouldn't show bloodstains.

"Johnny, today I want to tell you something I've never mentioned. Make yourself comfortable because there's a story attached."

"When isn't there a story?" I said with a smile. "Go ahead, sir."

He loved to talk about his life before Redmond, as though the young man he had once been was now understood by a gentler, wiser elder. He talked of his mistakes, some of them what he called "whoppers."

"I had no patience, Johnny, that was my one big flaw. I wanted everything right away." He'd said that both times. He said, "I don't hold that against myself, though. Growing up, I was the poor kid, the one whose family got the charity box from the Rotary Club every year. Grown up, I was a show-off—never drove a black car if I could get one fire-engine red. My wheels squealed around corners and my horn played 'Sweet Talkin' Guy.'"

He didn't tell me sob stories, nor did he make himself the hero of his tales. He just wanted me to know him. He wanted to know me too. Not really me—he'd never know *me*. But he wanted to know his son.

My real name is Brian Moore. I am Millie Moore's kid, one of these single-parent children. So in the beginning it sounded like fun to pretend I was Onondaga John's son.

My mother's bed-and-breakfast, called the Blue Moon, specializes in the families of men locked up in Redmond Prison, right in our downtown.

When you cater to a crowd of women (mostly) whose brothers or husbands or fathers are doing nickels and dimes, you get to know them. Onondaga John is doing two quarters, and of that fifty-year sentence he's served only sixteen years.

We call Mrs. Klee, his wife, Polly Posh, because there is something posh about her, something glamorous—even though, as she likes to say, her days of Concorde flights and mansions, silk sheets and chauffeurs, are over. She is a forty-eight-year-old con's wife. Her rich family want nothing to do with her. Neither does her son, the real Johnny. He moved in with his grandparents when he was eight years old. Now, at Oxford House, he tells his prep school pals that his dad is dead.

For a long while Onondaga John didn't want anything to do with his son either. He was ashamed of himself, and uncertain about how the boy felt toward him. Early in his sentence Polly had said something about not wanting to bring a little kid to Redmond Prison, not wanting to have him see his father that way. Onondaga John thought there was a possibility she'd lied to their boy, maybe said he was on some secret mission far away . . . maybe even said he was dead. It wasn't uncommon for prisoners' wives to keep the truth from their kids.

Onondaga John didn't even ask to see pictures of Johnny Jr. Let Polly bring up the boy the way she thought best.

He asked her if Johnny needed anything, if everything was okay with him—general references, but nothing specific. Polly guessed Onondaga John was too proud to face a little tyke walking through those iron doors, calling out "Daddy." Not *his* son! Leave well enough alone.

Polly was just as glad he felt that way. She never had to tell her husband that the boy had turned into Little Lord-It-Over-Everyone. She never had to tell Onondaga John that his son claimed to be fatherless.

Then came the fatal day when Onondaga John told Polly he'd like to meet his son. "Isn't he around sixteen now?"

"Yes." Polly told my mother she was thinking right then and there that *I* was around sixteen too.

"Does he know about me, Polly?"

"Yes."

"Bring him along next time. I'm not planning to become a daddy to him suddenly. I just want to see him."

"Sure," Polly said.

That night at the Blue Moon, Polly asked my mother and me, "What would it hurt if Brian visited him, said he was his son?"

"Well, Brian," said my mother, "here's your chance to be an actor. Here's your chance to prove to everyone at that school you're the Tom Hanks of Redmond, not some flop!"

"He can't *tell* anyone he's doing it!" said Polly. "And who said he was a flop?"

"That's what they think of him," said my mother. "Ask him."

"Why do they think that, Brian?" Polly asked me.

"Not every kid comes across as interesting. *I* don't." That was putting it mildly. I didn't "come across" at all, except as El Nerdo.

"This might make you *feel* interesting," Polly said, "even if you can't talk about it."

I said, "It'd be a change anyway."

I thought the main thing would be seeing inside Redmond. You live in a prison city your whole life never knowing what's behind those walls. You see the guys going and coming on the buses in and out of Redmond. Going with a birdcage and the shiny new suit the state pays for. Coming, manacled to a plainclothesman, not wanting to look you in the eye.

But the main thing didn't turn out to be Redmond Prison. It was Onondaga John himself. Right away he asked me how I felt about things, and he told me how *he* did. He said his favorite author was Charles Dickens and one of his favorite books was *Great Expectations*. What do you like to read, he wanted to know, and whose music do you like? What do you want to be someday? "An *actor*?" he said. "Hey! Hey!" he said, grinning at me, looking as pleased as though I'd just unlocked the front gate and said "You're free."

I'd never had an adult male interested in me unless it was a guidance counselor wanting to know why my fingernails were chewed down to the quick, or why I couldn't stop rubbing away my eyebrows.

I'm okay when I'm at the Blue Moon. I belong there, setting up the chips for the poker games, listening to old Mrs. Resnick cry that her hubby no sooner gets out than he goes right back in, answering the rattle of bells at the front door, always eager to see if it's someone new, someone whose relative we've seen on Court TV.

Everyone there likes me too. Everyone knows I'll sneak a peanut butter sandwich to them late at night. I'll let the cats up the back stairs to sleep with those who need a little fur and purr around their necks. I'll get them thrillers or romance books from the library with my card. I'll watch the spooky stuff on TV with them in our parlor, and I can sit in for card games too. Bridge, poker, and gin.

Follow me out of the Blue Moon, down two blocks and over three, and you've seen me land in enemy territory: Redmond High School.

Mousey Moore, on the short side with thin brown hair and bird legs, arms just as skinny.

At the Blue Moon I babble and crack jokes and listen and hum.

In that puke-yellow brick building with the flagpole out front, I am duh. I scurry down the halls like the mousey they've named me. Not even mouse. I am littler. My whiskers bristle with fear. My nostrils quiver. Inside, everything trembles.

"Hey, Mousey, did you bring a cheese sandwich for lunch?" Someone has tossed an empty Coke can at the back of my head.

"Did the mousey bring cheese for himself? Did you, Mousey?"

"Yis." I can't even make it sound like yes. It hisses out of me between chattering teeth: *Yisss.*

"Is the cat after you, Mousey?" I feel a sneaker press down on the back of my shoe.

"Nip." For nope—nip, and I skitter down the hall to get away, oh-oh, not in the boys', it'll be worse in there. Try by your locker. Just open the door and hide by your locker.

But there is no way for someone like me to hide at school.

I hide in my head, fantasizing that I've grown tall and strong enough to fight them. Or suddenly so unbelievably handsome and amusing they all long to be my friend.

I pray for days when something *big* is going on in the town or the world, taking their minds off me.

Now Onondaga John was at the end of his story, which was about his courtship of Polly Posh, how he adored her, and how frightened he was of Mr. Pullman, her father: rich and powerful, six foot three, with a booming voice. Pullman would look down his nose at John Klee and say things like "Don't wear brown shoes again, fellow. It's not a man's color."

"You don't know what that's like, do you, Johnny? To be scorned. Polly tells me you have lots of friends at your fancy school. What's its name?"

"Oxford House, sir."

"Yes. Your grandfather Pullman went there, and his father too."

"Yes, sir."

"Do you admire the Pullmans, Johnny?"

"Not really, sir." Not from what I'd heard about them! Polly said Johnny'd become so spoiled living there. He instructed the maids to remove all magazine inserts before putting them in his room. He only wore a terry-cloth robe once, then threw it out and grabbed a new one from the shelf in his bathroom. The entire Pullman family were wastrels, said Polly—greedy and ungiving.

Onondaga John said, "I was afraid you'd come under their influence, since you're their only grandchild. I'm glad you stuck with your mother!"

That was when he told me he was going to see that I received $240,000.

I swallowed hard. "But where would you get that much money, sir?"

"Let's say from a partner of mine, Johnny."

I had never asked him about the last bank robbery, though I did know it was the first time he had worked with partners. Before that he always went solo, and only robbed banks in Onondaga County, upstate New York.

There were three robbers in the Salina Bank robbery. I did know that one turned state witness and claimed Onondaga John shot the cop. Polly swore he never had, he *wouldn't,* it wasn't in him to kill anyone. Steal, yes! Kill, uh-uh!

The third man had apparently taken off with the loot from the heist.

"Johnny? You look slightly reluctant. It's not dirty money, Johnny. It doesn't belong to people. I've never robbed *people.* I've robbed banks, and banks reimburse depositors. Insurance is a business like any other, with its risks and gains. They bet someone like me won't come along. I bet someone like them won't be prepared when I do."

"I never thought of it that way." I'd never thought of it at all.

"This is just another little mystery story, Johnny." Sometimes at the end of a story he'd say that, then add, "Life is mysterious. You don't know that yet, but you'll see."

"It's very hard for me to believe," I told him.

"I plan to give you thirty thousand dollars a year for eight years," said Onondaga John. "Your first payment will come to the Blue Moon, in cash, in six months."

My mouth must have fallen open; my eyes must have been round with amazement.

"Don't say anything, Johnny, just listen. It will be yours to do with as you please. I like the way you've turned out. I trust you, Son. Unlike me, you have a noble heart you will *not* disgrace."

I don't know about a noble heart. Do you know what I thought I'd do first with the money? I would hire a drama student from Redmond University, where theater was featured. He would be big and tough looking, able to handle himself in any circumstance. I would buy a Saab convertible for him to drive. We would get some Redmond University coeds to accompany us.

We would appear at all the games together, at the dances, at Pizza Palace, all the places I never went, fearing the bullies would be there too.

I would no longer be Mousey Moore. Moose, maybe. The Moose.

"We can't take that money," said my mother. "Brian, what could you be thinking of? Stolen money? It's bad luck, honey!"

"He didn't offer it to *us*, Mom. He offered it to me. I can take it." I gave her Onondaga John's explanation about insurers being businessmen, about risks attached to business.

"Malarkey!" she said. "That's how Onondaga John got where he is!"

That night after the poker game Polly said she was going back the next afternoon.

"Then send us an E-mail that Johnny's been hit by a two-ton truck," said my mother. "We are ready to end this charade."

"Not me," I said. "I'm not ready."

"I can't say that I blame you, Brian," Polly said. "Now I understand why John wanted to meet his son. He told me what he's planning. Better you than the real Johnny! And I'll expect to be a nonpaying lodger after you get your first installment."

"If that money comes to this house, it'll go right back!" said my mother.

"Go right back where?" Polly said. "Apparently the third man is dying, and he's already put the cash somewhere in John's name."

"We won't have any trouble getting someone to take it away," said my mother. "Particularly someone in navy blue with a silver badge."

"That's a lot of money," said Polly.

"You keep it if you love having stolen money so much," said my mother.

Polly gave me a wink. She said, "What boy couldn't use some new clothes and music and something like a little Saab to get around in?"

"Convertible," I said. "A Saab convertible."

By the time Polly left, she had jollied my mother into thinking about it.

But my mother did ask me, "What kind of values do you have that you think it's important to have new clothes, new music, and a new Saab?"

"Convertible," I said. "A new Saab convertible."

"What kind of values are those?"

"Teenage values," I said.

"Do they teach you that at school?"

"They don't have to," I said. "It's our job to know it."

Suddenly, back at school, this girl who was head of the drama club asked me if I would be in a play.

She can see the change in me already, I decided. I had a suspicion there was a new spring to my step and I might even have grown an inch since the thought that $240,000 could be mine . . . soon.

Polly had kissed me good-bye and said hang in there, we'll work on Mom. I somehow could not believe my mother, upright and honest as she is, would really not go to sleep thinking of things we could have with $30,000 a year to spend. We needed a computer, since ours from the early eighties had finally crashed, and we needed a third bathroom, and we needed new poker chips. We were not unneedy at the Blue Moon.

I told the President of the Redmond High School Players Club that of course I would accept a role in the play. How many times had I tried out for parts that always went to someone else?

Making myself sound no more excited than I imagined Leonardo DiCaprio might be, offered a movie role, I asked what the play was called.

"What You Really Are Is What You Don't Eat," she said. "It's an original comedy about food fads.'"

"What's my part?" I knew I wouldn't be the lead. It didn't matter. It was a beginning.

"You'll be a rabbit. You know how your nostrils vibrate sometimes, Mousey?"

So there was *not* a new spring to my step, new growth, or anything new to accompany the visions I had of cars and travel and college campuses spread out over lush green hills, some sweaters (cashmere), pants, coats, toss a cap in, keep going, keep going.

I was still not quite human by the standards at RHS. But I had progressed from a rodent to a hare.

That afternoon on my way from school I was tripped, pushed, made to flush like a toilet on the circular cement walk, and warned that life was short for shorties. Just another day in Paradise.

Ah, but then, as Onondaga John liked to say, Fate frolicked

into the picture. Walking along Genesee Street, I saw the spanking-new Marshall Sylvester Saab Center. In the window was a beige convertible with beige leather seats.

I made a casual entrance—just slipped inside, you might say—and sidled over for a look-see.

"You're the kid from the Blue Moon," Mr. Sylvester said. "I remember you used to come into my showroom on Jefferson Avenue and say you just wanted to have a look-see. I don't spend the day in a suit and tie to talk to little squirts about cars!"

"I'm not looking for myself. I'm looking for Johnny Klee Jr. Ever hear of him? He's inherited a fortune."

"No, I never heard of him. You *are* the kid from the Blue Moon, though, aren't you?"

"So what? I'm not always going to be the kid from the Blue Moon. My friend, Johnny Klee, goes to Oxford House, in Boston, Mass. And he would prefer to have brown leather seats in his convertible, not those beige ones."

"Yeah, yeah. Tell him to come in. Who did he inherit the fortune from?"

"His father."

"Klee? From around here?"

"Did I say from around here?"

"Tell him brown leather seats will take eight weeks."

"We'll wait."

"Yeah, yeah. How's business at the Blue Moon? With all these dope addicts being sent up for grand theft and manslaughter, your mother must be rich."

"The one who's rich," I said, "is my buddy, Johnny Klee Jr."

There are people you just can't impress, and that seemed

to be the case with Marshall Sylvester. I slunk out of the show-room trying to whistle nonchalantly, telling myself: *So what!*

I couldn't go to Redmond Prison just anytime at all. I had to wait for Polly to come to town. But my thoughts were on Onondaga John. When I wasn't thinking of new things I would buy for myself, I would find something somewhere that John Klee would like: a tin of those Altoid peppermints he favored; Old English aftershave; a rhyming dictionary, since he told me he wrote poetry. I even found him a leather-bound copy of *Great Expectations*. It was an interesting story for me to read at this point in my life, for it was about a boy who also had "great expectations" of money. I was going to be a grateful and atten-tive recipient. I was going to be a son.

"Is Mrs. Moore in?" the guy said.

"She'll be right back," I said, looking him over, figuring he was probably in Redmond to see a brother or a father, his first time, shy about saying why he was there. Someone had given him the address of the Blue Moon, even though we were known to favor female clients. We liked help in the kitchen, clean bathrooms, anything but sports on the big TV in the parlor—and other things along those lines that a male clientele did not guarantee.

"Sit down," I said. "You don't have to stand."

"I like to stand," he said. He was one of those. How dare *I* suggest a course of action *he* should take?

I slung my schoolbooks on the couch in our parlor and took a good look at this long young man. The teeniest, tiniest gold stud in his left ear, black hair, probably shoulder length, tied back with a bit of leather.

"If you're planning to stay here," I said, "I can sign you in."

"I don't know if I'm staying or not. I'd like to know about the visiting hours at the . . . ahem . . . um . . . prison here in town."

"Tomorrow you can visit between noon and three," I said.

"Then I'm forced to stay, I guess."

"I'll sign you in," I said, crossing to my mother's small desk. "Your name?"

"John Pullman," he said.

"John . . . *Pullman*." Of course. He had taken his grandparents' name.

"I want to stay on a smoke-free floor, in a room with a view and a comfortable chair with arms, a private bath, and a double bed."

If I had imagined in my wildest dreams how the real Johnny would look and act, it would be exactly as the real Johnny looked and acted. Preppies always seem more confident, and feel free to order you around.

"Another thing." I found out this was a favorite way for him to begin sentences. "Can you tell me anything about Marshall Sylvester?"

"He's the Saab dealer here," I said.

"Yes, so he announced when he called Oxford House looking for Johnny Klee. I haven't been called that since I was eight years old! When it came over the intercom I about had a duck!"

He looked down at me and his lips tipped into a snide, lopsided grin. "And you must be the kid from the Blue Moon who said I'd prefer brown leather seats to beige ones in my new convertible."

"The beige are harder to keep clean," I said, everything

inside me sinking to my shoes, heart pounding, nervous breakdown suggestions throughout my terminals.

"Another thing," he barked, "what do you know about my father leaving me money?"

"I was just kidding," I croaked. People really do croak in dire circumstances. I learned that.

"What do you know about that old jailbird? What do you know about the third man?" He bent down so that he could look me in the eye. "And how does my mother fit into this picture?"

What would be the ending to this story? Onondaga John might ask, if he was telling it. And is this a story about who gets the money, or is it a story about what the thought of getting the money can do?

Perhaps it's both. As Onondaga John would point out, there are many levels to the best stories, and in life there are levels galore!

The thought of getting the money did not make much of a dent on Polly Posh, though she was curious about where it came from.

My mother reacted to the thought of getting the money with hostile threats.

Marshall Sylvester went to his computer as he thought of getting the money, and was able to locate a Saab dealer in Mattituck, New York, with a convertible, in stock, complete with brown leather seats. He made a phone call to Oxford House.

The thought of anyone else getting the money brought the real Johnny to Redmond, finally, to meet his father.

No one but the fly on the wall knows what was said between the two. It was the first and last visit.

Now me. The thought of getting the money made me strut away from duh and yissss and nip for whatever brief time. True, I was propelled by borrowed glory, and there are finer places than the Marshall Sylvester Saab Showroom to boast in . . . and a more receptive audience than the cynical and sarcastic Sylvester himself. But I don't take that blame, for I was new to the promise of a windfall—impatient and flawed.

I *did* write a story about it, in the style of Onondaga John: Sit back, relax, and I'll tell you a mistake I made—a whopper!

"The Fool in the Saab Showroom" was its title.

It was the only A+ that I ever received in any subject, and across the top my English teacher wrote: "How interesting! What an imagination!"

"Hey, Mousey!" a kid yelled at me as I hurried home from the trenches and minefields of RHS. "Where'd you steal that story from?"

Then there was a chorus: *Is there any cure for poor Mouse Moore?*

Instead of provoking respect in my predators, I inspired them to reach a new creative height: *rhyming.*

One day there was a postcard on my bed, where Mother left all mail: on people's beds. It said:

Thanks for the look at your story, Brian! You're a better actor than a writer, in my opinion, but then I saw you act three times, and this is the only story of yours I've read.

If it's good enough to be included in your school literary magazine that should tell you something.

Out of our biggest difficulties, we make our little songs.

Do I mind that you put me in a story, you ask? It is the only justification I can think of for deceiving me. So I don't mind. You wouldn't have had a story without me.

I gave you a lot of material, so in a sense, you have great expectations, after all. (Thanks for the book etc.)

Here's my advice to you: Use it all. Keep on writing. Use everything that comes your way.

Farewell, J.K.

No one I know ever found out what became of the money from the third man, not even Polly Posh.

John Klee would say, "This is just another little mystery story. Life is mysterious. You don't know that yet, but you'll see."

And of course those schoolmates of mine are right: There is no cure for poor Mouse Moore.

They will always be coming after me.

They are what I have come to expect.

I'LL SEE YOU
WHEN THIS WAR IS OVER

I was thirteen the winter everything changed. I knew, even on the cold December night Bud left, that our family would never be the same again. Everyone was at the dinner table: Bud, me, Mom, Dad, my other brother, Tommy, and Hope Hart, from the next town over, Doylestown, Pennsylvania.

No one was saying anything except what began with *Please pass the . . .* I hated the way no one would talk about it, but not enough to mention it myself. Someone had left the radio on in the living room. We could hear Radio Dan signing off. He was a Number One cornball, but I listened to him sometimes, secretly. He was the only celebrity I had a personal acquaintance with, never mind he wasn't always sure which Shoemaker kid I was. He lived down at the end of our street. He had this deep, friendly voice. You'd think he'd understand anything you told him. But I knew better. Radio Dan wouldn't understand what Bud was doing, that was for sure.

My father got up, went in, and turned him off. He hardly ever listened to the radio anymore. Everything was about the war.

A rib roast, Bud's favorite, was being slowly eaten in

silence. Even Mahatma, our old collie, who favored Bud over all of us, seemed to sense something dire was taking place. He lay just outside the dining room, his eyes fixed on Bud.

When we finally left the house to take Bud to his train, Mom was crying and hanging on to him. Bud didn't want her to see him off. She said she'd send him some of her gingerbread and macaroons.

"I don't even know if we can get packages from home," Bud said.

"Of course you can!" Mom said.

Dad said, "Maybe he can't. We don't know how they feel about it."

"Well, he's not going to prison, Ef."

"No, he's not, and he's not going to Boy Scout camp, either."

"Ef, what a mean thing to say!"

"I didn't mean it mean."

"Don't send me anything, okay?" Bud said.

Mom cried out, "Come inside, Mahatma! You can't go with him!"

I thought I'd be the one to ride in back with Bud. I couldn't get used to Bud having a steady girl. He'd been with Hope almost two years, but I kept thinking it was like a case of measles or chicken pox—it'd go away in a while.

"Jubal, ride up here with me and Tom," Dad said.

Tommy put the radio on.

In the back of the Buick, Bud and Hope were sitting so close you'd think there were passengers on either side of them. They were holding hands. Earlier that evening, Hope had given Bud a silver identification bracelet with their initials on the front and "Mind the Light" on the inside.

Hope Hart was a goody two-shoes and an optimist, the kind whose sunny ways wore you down eventually. She had hair a color in between red and brown, and brown eyes. She always knew the right way to walk in and out of rooms, and what to say in them. It was a skill Bud didn't have. He scowled his way through most social gatherings.

Hope was a year older than Bud, and she already had a college degree in home economics. I wanted to like her. I didn't want to blame her for everything that was happening to Bud.

I could hear Hope whispering to Bud, "I love thee. I'll wait for thee, Bud, for as long as need be."

"And I love thee."

They were speaking the old-fashioned "plain language" some Friends still used with family and at Meetings.

Nobody in our family used it until Bud met Hope when he took the summer job on their farm. After that I would hear Bud speak it nights on the telephone. *I think of thee all the time.*

As a young man, Dad did not think of himself as a strict Quaker. He wasn't a regular at the Meeting House. His family way back was, and then he was when he met my mother. Tommy was a lot like Dad used to be. But Bud and I were believers. We would never have considered a school that wasn't Quaker. Bud ultimately chose to go to Swarthmore College. Sometimes when he was home and would speak at Sweet Creek Meeting, I would hear how serious he was about religion. I would be surprised at Bud's anger, telling off Friends there, saying they were some of the most successful businessmen in the county, but did they tithe, did they give 10 percent of their earnings to Friends? Bud bet not! His eyes were fire, and I would be amazed. I also worried that I wasn't as strong as Bud. When it came my time to register for the draft, what kind of a Quaker would I be?

My dad said that it was a good thing Bud had found Hope. Hope, he had said, was more like Bud than Bud was.

"Remember Pearl Harbor," a male chorus sang on the radio.

Dad snapped, "Shut that off!"

"I'll change the station," Tommy said.

"It'll be the same everywhere," Dad grumbled.

Tommy tried, got "Here Comes Santa Claus," tried again and got "White Christmas," tried again and got some news commentator saying the making of automobiles had stopped and the factories were being changed over to airplane and tank factories. In a short time the making of new radios for home use would be cut in half because the materials were needed for the war. Rubber, tin, and aluminum had become precious and were being saved for only the most important uses. Men's suits—

"Turn it off, Tom!"

"Yes sir."

I glanced up at Tommy, and he gave me a weak smile. He was seventeen. Bud was twenty. I was the baby. But all of us looked alike. We all had thick black hair, sturdy builds, and the Shoemaker light blue eyes.

Anyone in Sweet Creek could spot us as Efram Shoemaker's kids. E.F. SHOEMAKER was the sign over the only department store in town. My father called himself E.F. because he'd never liked the name Efram. Most people called him that, anyway. If you never liked the name, why did you give it to Bud? I asked him once. Tradition, the answer came back. There'd been an Efram Shoemaker in Delaware County since the 1600s. Bud was Efram Elam Shoemaker. "Elam" after our grandfather, just as I was Jubal after our great-great-grandfather. Lucky for Tommy that our great-grandfather was named Thomas.

While my father parked the car, Tommy, Hope, Bud, and I went into the station.

When everyone sat down, I asked Bud, "Aren't you going to get a ticket?"

"I already have a ticket, Jube."

"When did you get it?"

"The government's paying his way," Tommy said.

"They are?" I was surprised. I thought that was the last thing the government would do: spring for a ticket for a conscientious objector.

"How long do you have to wait in New York before your train to Colorado?" Hope said. She was wearing her long hair pageboy style. She was in a red plaid pleated skirt with boots and a white turtleneck sweater under a navy blue pea jacket.

"It's just a few hours' wait," Bud said.

"But what will you do at this time of night?" Hope asked.

Bud tried a grin but didn't quite manage it. "There's always something to do in New York," he said, making it sound as though he knew all there was to know about Manhattan. He'd only been there once, years ago, for a Boy Scout jamboree.

Tommy said, "You could call Aunt Lizzy."

"I don't think she'd want me to call her," Bud said.

"Sure she would. You were always her favorite."

"Was," said Bud. "Now, who knows?"

Dad came in from the parking lot, and right behind him was Radio Dan and his kid.

If you didn't know Dan Daniel, you'd never expect that big, deep voice.

In person, Radio Dan was plump and medium-height, balding, with a beer belly. He always wore polka-dot bow ties, blue ones, green ones, yellow ones. Were they clip-ons? He liked to wear V-neck sleeveless sweaters, the same color, with them.

"Shhhoot!" Tommy said. "Radio Dan and Dean!"

"So act like who cares," I said.

"Who does care?" Bud shrugged.

Everyone seemed to be saying good-bye at railroad or bus stations those days. There were uniforms everywhere. Some of the guys wearing them looked to me like kids dressed up to play war games in their backyards.

That's what Dean Daniel looked like that evening—this skinny boy dressed up like a marine. His ears stuck out at the sides of his cap. He'd been my junior counselor in Cub Scout camp one summer, but he'd called for his folks to come and get him because he was terrified of spiders. Dean was a twin, but when you saw him with Danny Jr., they didn't even look like brothers. Danny Jr. looked tough, and he was.

The Daniels waved at us and sat down on a bench nearby. Radio Dan was lighting a cigarette and passing the pack to Dean.

My father's ears were red. I'd always thought he wasn't comfortable with what Bud was doing. He'd never said as much, but I had overheard conversations between Mom and him, and I'd heard him say he wasn't sure he would have made the same decision.

"Is the train on time?" Dad asked Tommy. His voice was so low, Tommy had to ask him what he said.

He said it again, then shuffled his feet and stole a glance back at the Daniels.

Everyone in Sweet Creek knew about Bud, particularly Radio Dan. He knew all the town gossip. Nothing was secret for long in a town of twenty thousand. Bud had been asked not to lead his Boy Scout troop last fall. When he drove up at Texaco in his old Ford with the "A" gas-rationing sticker on the windshield, the help took their time coming out to collect his coupon and gas him up. It was the same when he stopped at Sweet Creek Diner for coffee, or went into Acme Food Stores for groceries. No one wanted to be of service to Bud Shoemaker.

"Please don't wait for the train," Bud said.

"We want to wait with you, Bud," Dad said.

"We're waiting," said Tommy.

"I don't want you to wait," Bud said.

I sang a little of "Wait 'Til the Sun Shines, Nellie," trying to provide some comic relief. But I knew there was no such thing as relief for Bud's situation. It was just going to get worse every day the war lasted.

I went into the Men's, and Tommy followed me.

"I bet Dad hates having Radio Dan here!" Tommy said.

I knew that Tommy hated it, too. Dean was home on leave from boot camp in Parris Island, South Carolina. His twin had joined the marines when he was seventeen.

A few days ago, Tommy and I had run into Dean in town in front of the bank. He was with his kid sister, Darie, her hair soft and tawny. She was my age but older-looking and -acting, the way girls have of becoming people before boys do. She didn't bother to greet me, just stood there regarding me with these cool, bored eyes, as though in her short time on this planet she had rarely been subjected to an encounter with anyone as ordinary as I was.

Dean punched his palm with his fist and told us he couldn't wait to kill a Jap. Then he covered his mouth with his hand and said, "Whoops! Wrong guy to tell that to!"

Tommy shrugged and said, "I'm not partial to Japs."

"You'd never kill one, I bet!" Darie Daniel piped up. She was always in Sweet Creek High plays, particularly ones with music. Twice a night there was a recording of her singing Radio Dan's theme song. I'd seen her in a few Gilbert and Sullivan operettas. She was cocky, a little tomboyish, and she could belt a song so you'd hear it down to City Hall.

Folks went past us, in and out of the bank. Tommy answered, "I doubt I'd ever kill anyone."

"Even if someone was holding a gun to your mother's head?" Darie Daniel said. "What would you do then?"

"I'd sic my bulldog here on him." Tommy ruffled my hair and grinned down at me.

Bud had told us the draft board asked him those kind of questions. *What would you do if you saw a man raping a woman? What if foreign invaders came on your street; would you help fight them?*

"Let's drop the subject," Dean said. "It's the last thing I want to talk about when I'm home on leave."

"I know how to shoot a gun," Darie Daniel said. "And I'd

have no compunction about blasting away if anyone dared
hurt a member of my family!"

That night while he washed his hands beside me in the
Men's, Tommy muttered, "Radio Dan's going to mention
this, wait and see!"

"Probably," I agreed.

"At least Darie wasn't with them," Tommy said.

"Who cares about Darie?"

"I go to the same school with her! You don't!"

"It's Bud I feel sorry for," I said. "Did you notice Radio
Dan said all our names but his?"

When we came back out, Tommy checked on Bud's train and
called out, "Track three. All aboard, Bud!"

The Daniels got up, too. There was only one train heading
for Manhattan.

Suddenly, servicemen seemed to come from everywhere,
all heading for track three.

Dad stopped and held up his hand. "We'll say our goodbyes
here."

He hugged Bud and then Tommy did.

"I'll miss you, Bud," I said.

Bud bent down and held me tight. "I'll see you when this
war is over. You take care of Mom," he said.

"Okay, I will."

"I'll write you from Colorado," Bud told us.

Radio Dan and his boy had stopped a few feet away.

"Take care of yourself, son!" that fabulous voice rang out.

After our good-byes, we left Hope standing alone with
Bud, locked in this long kiss, and headed for the exit.

Radio Dan was also headed toward the only exit there was.

Because Bud was a conscientious objector, he was going to a Civilian Public Service Camp. But I was still in the dark about what would become of him next. I had the feeling he didn't know himself.

Last fall, he'd received a list of things he should pack. There was everything there from "two pairs of medium-weight long underwear with long sleeves and legs" to "three bed sheets good quality, at least 63 by 99 inches."

Radio Dan paused to light another cigarette.

"What's going to happen to Bud now?" I asked my father, keeping my voice down. "Will he have a job?"

"Wait until we get home."

E. F. Shoemaker Company and radio station WBEA were on the same side of Pilgrim Lane, a few doors from each other. Tuesdays Dad and Radio Dan went to Rotary together. Before Rotary, Dad would stop by the radio station to pick up Radio Dan and walk down to Sweet Creek Inn with him for the luncheon meeting.

And there the two of them were at the train station: one seeing his second son off to war, and Dad seeing Bud off to Colorado, about as far away from any war as he could get.

When Hope caught up with us, for the first time her eyes had a watery look, but she was holding her chin up, smiling.

She said, "Bud's going to be fine!" Then, probably for Radio Dan's benefit, "I'm so proud of him!"

"Well, we all are, we all are," Dad said in a voice so low we could hardly hear it.

The four of us walked silently to the car, not talking, until Tommy suddenly blurted out, "This damn, damn war!"

THE FIRE AT FAR AND AWAY

Around here they still talk about the fire at Far and Away. That small landmark cottage on the point of the bay, burned to the ground. Fishermen going for clams waded ashore and watched helplessly. My father was gone by then. Everybody said he'd set the fire. He used to work at Far and Away. He used to open his big mouth mornings he was getting coffee at Springs Store, nearby. He'd laugh about his bosses and call them names. I can hear him now.

"Ah, it's spring and the pansies are back," my father said. He was checking our phone machine messages. "What do they want me to do now? Put a tub of posies out by their mailbox?"

I never said anything when Dad made fun of Paul and Robert. It made my life a lot easier than if I'd ever let on to him that I didn't think they were bad guys at all. The few times I'd been to Far and Away they didn't seem any different from other New Yorkers who came to spend the summer in our town.

I remember once I called them a couple and Dad blew.

"Don't call them that! Your mother and I were a *couple*! They're fakes! They're phonies!"

After Dad erased the messages on our phone machine, he said "This job at Far and Away has your name on it, Sonny Boy. They want their house opened."

"Why does it have *my* name on it?"

"You're the neatnik. I'm not as good at dusting as you are, either."

I let him get away with a lot. If I didn't, he'd see an opening and go in after me. He'd call me Girl instead of Gil. He'd make fun of my idea to be a chef one day. He'd go for the throat, as only Dad and his buddies could when they thought they saw a weakness in someone.

My dad called himself a contractor, but he was really a carpenter, a plumber, a yard man—he did what work came his way. He was more than an unskilled laborer but not much more. None of the men he hung out with ever went to college and like Dad, some of them never finished high school.

You can imagine how they resented the rich gay fellows who have summer homes here. Double it where my father was concerned. He was afraid his own son had tendencies.

Before my mother died he'd tell her I was beginning to look as pretty as her when they first started dating. I did have her blue eyes, and there were a few summers my blond hair was long. I liked to bake and I *was* a self-proclaimed neatnik. That was all Dad needed, to get on my back, when he was tired and depressed. Then he'd call me "Girlie" and he'd see if he could make me mad.

I felt so sorry for him, the way he missed Mom, and sorry for me the way I missed her, too. I let him say things Mom would have left the room over.

•　　•　　•

Now I have to confess something even Dad didn't know. It happened the summer before the fire. I'd worked as a waiter/ bus boy for a big party Paul and Robert gave at Far and Away.

I was just fourteen. They were paying me fifteen dollars an hour to pass trays of food and keep the floors and tables clear of empty glasses and dishes. I wore a white jacket and black pants, a white shirt and a black bow tie.

I'd pop shrimp into my mouth before I passed a tray around. I tasted the baked clams, the raw oysters, and I had a hamburger and a hot dog fresh from the grill a cook tended in the back yard. There was that thin salmon, caviar, all the rich cheeses, then tiny pastries you could pick up in your hand. Or you could have big slices of chocolate cake, or key lime pie you could eat with a fork, sitting down somewhere to enjoy the string quartet playing on the terrace.

I was looking good and feeling good, just as though I was at parties like that one all the time. There were piles of throw-away cameras on trays in case anyone felt like having a photographic record of the evening. There were sterling silver key chains for souvenirs with round silver discs that said Far and Away.

Right in the middle of things I saw this wad of money held together by a gold dollar sign, on the floor of the hall closet.

I picked it up, took it into bathroom, and counted $100x10. $1000 smackeroos.

I put it in my pocket. I'd give it to Paul or Robert before the evening was over, I decided.

But it also occurred to me that no one could have seen

me. And who walks around with $1000 in his pocket at a party? Somebody who'd probably never miss it.

I wasn't a bad kid. For one thing Mom had been too sick for me to give her more to worry about. I studied, took odd jobs afternoons and summers to make spending money and buy my own clothes.

Money was always a problem. Dad and I talked about it all the time. How much we had for this, what we couldn't have, and what there was so far in my college fund.

Dad said, "You're going to college if I have to rob a bank."

"Things aren't that desperate," I said.

"Don't kid yourself, Gil."

The house Paul and Robert lived in was really a cottage. It was two hundred years old and it had been "fixed" by men like Dad time and again. One year during a hurricane, the bay rose and water came into the first floor. Dad said they spent a fortune repairing it, that they could have built a new house for what it cost. But it was one of those historic places. The original owner wouldn't sell it until he found buyers he trusted to keep it the way it was.

It only had two baths and three bedrooms. It faced the bay, no near neighbors, but beautiful gardens on both sides, mostly Robert's handiwork. My father used to say that you could tell which one took the garbage out in that house: it was Pauline, as he liked to call Paul. Roberta, Dad said, was the one with his nose in the daffodils and his hands in the salad bowl.

"Don't leave yet, Gil," Robert said that first night I worked there.

I waited until the last guest was out the door. I was sitting on the terrace, looking at the moon's reflection in the water, wishing we didn't live in such a crappy house, dad leaving his clothes where he took them off, never washing a dish, never giving a damn how anything looked.

"You had a rough winter, didn't you, Gil?" Robert said from behind me.

Then Paul said, "We liked your mom a lot, Gil. We're so sorry."

"Yeah. She liked you guys, too." Mom had helped out at Far and Away nights they had dinner parties, but the three of them had had a kind of friendship, too. She'd given them cuttings from plants and they'd brought by lilac bushes or dwarf evergreens. Once, Paul gave her some goldfish complete with fancy bowl. Our cat ate them that very evening, but we never let Paul and Robert know.

They had sent a couple dozen white roses to the funeral home and later they wrote Dad and me saying how much they'd cared for her. Enclosed was a photograph of Mom stretched out on a chaise in their yard, with their black toy poodle in her arms.

I could feel the money clip in my pants pocket. I was thinking of all the stuff I could get with it. I'd never be able to put it in the college fund because Dad would want to know where I got it. But I could use it for special occasions, special treats.

I couldn't believe that Robert was smiling so sweetly yet asking me "Do you want to return the gold clip you found, Gil?"

I was about to deny it but Paul said, "We were going to pay the help with that tonight. Then I saw *you* pick it up."

I could feel how hot my face and ears were. I took the clip out of my pocket and handed it to Robert.

I mumbled, "I meant to give it to you, then I forgot."

"Bull!" said Paul.

"What?" I was surprised at the sharp tone of voice.

"I said bull! You were going to walk off with it!"

"Don't be harsh, Paul," said Robert.

"When he stops lying and starts apologizing, I'll stop being harsh, not before!"

I heard myself let out this big sigh and say, "Paul's right. I was going to keep the money. I'm very sorry."

"Apology accepted," said Paul.

"Thanks," I said. "I guess I'll never be asked to work for you again."

"Sure you will," Robert said. "It's over and forgotten."

Paul drove me home.

He didn't say anything until the car stopped. Then he said, "Want to hear my rules for a good life?"

"Okay."

"Keep your body clean and your head clear and earn your own money."

I gave him a guilty smile and said thanks.

They weren't out from the city yet that afternoon I rode my bike over to open their house.

Enchanted Waters had already opened the little round pool in back. It was an unusually hot day for May, and I'd decided I'd take a swim later.

They had the kind of house that was a maid's dream. You had to look hard for any dust. I mostly opened and cleaned windows, and I mopped the kitchen floor. The funny thing was I liked to clean. I was good at it. I was fussy about my own things, too: my clothes, my room. I liked to try and create one little perfect area in our jungle house where I could be peaceful and forget what was in the other rooms.

When I had finished my housework at Far and Away, I shed my jeans, and T-shirt and took a swim. Then I flopped down in the rope hammock and enjoyed an eyes-shut daydream of owning this place, of having a gorgeous wife and well behaved, great looking kids who were off at the beach.

"Well! Well! Well! Our little Girlie is having herself a sunbath."

"And you've had a few beers, hmmm, Dad?"

"You walk around in your underwear here?"

"I went for a swim."

"Where are Pauline and Roberta?"

"We're right behind you, Mike." And there they were suddenly, and there was my father red-faced but with that defended posture, hands on hips, jaw stuck out, speechless for once. Furious, again—that pointless, humongous fury smoking away inside him ever since Mom died. I wasn't afraid of him, but I knew not to count on him anymore.

"Hello, Gil," Paul said, and Robert asked me "Is the water warm?"

"He's coming home with me now!" said Dad.

"Water's fine," I said.

"Get your clothes on, Girlie!" Dad said.

I said, "I'm coming."

"I don't want him swimming here!" Dad said. He was shaking his fist at them.

Paul said, "Whatever."

"Hey, Dad," I said, "Dad, for Pete's sake."

"What is whatever supposed to mean?" Dad demanded.

"It means whatever you say, that's fine," Paul said.

"You bet it is!" Dad said. "He's my son!"

"Cool it, Dad," I said. "I'm coming."

"He only *works* for you," Dad said, "and you remember that!"

"Not to worry, Mike," said Robert.

Then Dad said, "Wipe that smirk off of your face!" and went for Robert. And knocked Robert down.

Blood was running from a corner of Robert's mouth.

"You get out!" Paul shouted. "Get out now!"

"C'mon, Dad," I said. "C'mon, it's time to go."

Dad wasn't all bad, believe me. The next day he felt terrible about punching Robert. He told me I should go over there and give them his apologies, and before I could do it, he said no, he'd go himself.

He called them up to be sure they'd be there, and he drove off after bragging that he was an honorable man and an honorable man always owned up to his mistakes.

"Let that be a lesson to you," he said.

"Let it be a lesson to *you*," I said. "Don't lose your cool."

The thing was Dad stopped off for a few beers to work up the courage an honorable man needed. When he got over there, Paul and Robert were gone.

"Hey, Gilly boy?" he shouted at me over the phone. "I'm alone here at Far and Away. I've got an idea!"

"What, Dad? You've had a few beers again, haven't you?"

I could always tell by his voice when he'd been drinking.

"Before I got here I stopped off to do some thinking. You're right about not losing my cool, son. We need the work."

"And they've been darn nice to us, Dad."

"You're right," he admitted after a short pause. "Your mother liked them . . . So I'm going to do them a favor over here and you could help me."

"What are you going to do?"

"I'm going to paint that little kitchen of theirs without charge. I've got that can of white enamel in my truck and I just had it rotated yesterday."

"Dad, they may have their own ideas about it."

"Naw, no, they spoke before about painting that little room. Paint's peeling in there. I know what I'm doing."

"All right," I said. "I'll come over just so you don't mess it up!"

No surprise: Dad was sleeping in the rope hammock when I got there. He'd only finished one wall.

"What was destroyed was priceless," said Paul. "We saved for years and year to buy the Pollack painting. We couldn't afford to insure it."

"Our family photographs, our books, oh, everything," Robert said. "Everything. And this house . . . This house."

"Where is your father now?" the policeman asked me.

"He took off. The fire was raging and he just got into his pickup and went for help."

"Why did he set the fire?"

"He *didn't*," I said. "Why don't you listen to the truth?"

"Gil," Paul said, "don't protect him."

"*I* set the fire!"

They still wouldn't hear that.

Robert said, "Mike claimed he was coming here to tell us something. He sounded furious!"

"That's just his way," I said. "He knew he was wrong! He was going to apologize."

"Let's go downtown," said the policeman. "Let's get all the facts straight."

All the while I painted the kitchen that afternoon, I thought of how Dad ruined things, of what a ruin he was himself since Mom had died, of how I didn't think I could stand living any longer with damn Dad, out there snoring in the hammock!

I was mad! You bet I was mad!

But I worked on the ceiling, even while I was cursing my father. I was careful, too, neatnik that I am, I'd covered everything around me so paint wouldn't get on it.

I put newspapers down to keep the stove and the icebox clean.

I was about to do the last wall when I went out in the yard to shake my father and tell him he had to wake up and help! It was *his* idea to do them this favor, not mine!

The thing was, I'd never thought about that old gas stove. We had an electric stove, and so did everyone I knew.

While I was out yelling at Dad, the pilot light on the stove must have worked through the newspapers.

"I'm not going to paint anymore until you get up!" I told Dad.

"Who said you had to paint?" He had one eye open.

"You called me for help, remember?"

"I changed my mind." He turned over in the hammock, his back to me.

The fire must have been running along the walls just as I sat down in the beach chair and said, "Have it your way, Dad."

I don't know if he heard me.

But soon we both heard the whoooosh and then the roar of the fire as it hit the propane gas tanks.

I can't stand to drive down Bay Street and see the lick of land where Far and Away used to be.

Robert and Paul are long gone from this town now, but in my mind's eye, I still see their shocked, sad faces as we stood out on the lawn that sunny afternoon, the smell of burnt wood in the air, what was left of the house black and smoking.

Everyone, including them, still believe my father set that fire somehow, even though I figured out how it started, and later an inspector from the fire department confirmed it.

There are certain truths no one wants to hear. No one can believe truths that are hard to accept, either.

For example, who would ever believe that the real reason Far and Away burned down was that my father was trying to do a favor for Robert and Paul?

A PERSONAL HISTORY
BY M. E. KERR

My real name is Marijane Meaker.

When I first came to New York City from the University of Missouri, I wanted to be a writer. To be a writer back then, one needed to have an agent. I sent stories out to a long list of agents, but no one wanted to represent me. So, I decided to buy some expensive stationery and become my own agent. All of my clients were me with made-up names and backgrounds. "Vin Packer" was a male writer of mystery and suspense. "Edgar and Mamie Stone" were an elderly couple from Maine who wrote confession stories. (They lived far away, so editors would not invite them for lunch.) "Laura Winston" wrote short stories for magazines like *Ladies' Home Journal*. "Mary James" wrote only for Scholastic. Her bestseller is *Shoebag*, a book about a cockroach who turns into a little boy.

My most successful writer was Vin Packer. I wrote twenty-one paperback suspense novels as Packer. When I wanted to take credit for these books, my editor told me I could not, because Vin Packer was the bestselling author—not Marijane Meaker.

I was friends with Louise Fitzhugh—author of *Harriet the Spy*—who lived near me in New York City. We often took time away from our writing to have lunch, and we would gripe about writing being such hard work. Louise would claim that writing suspense novels was easier than writing for children because you could rob and murder and include other "fun things." I'd answer that children's writing seemed much easier; describing adults from a kid's eye, writing about school and siblings—there was endless material.

I asked Louise what children's book she would recommend, and she said I'd probably like Paul Zindel's *The Pigman*, a book for children slightly older than her audience. I did like it, a lot, and I decided my next book would be a teenage one (at the time, we didn't use the term "YA" to describe that genre). I knew I would need yet another pseudonym for this venture, so I invented one, a take-off on my last name, Meaker: M. E. Kerr. (Louise, on the other hand, never tried to write for adults. She was a very good artist, and her internal quarrel was whether to be a writer or a painter.)

Dinky Hocker Shoots Smack! was my first Kerr novel. The story of an overweight and sassy fifteen-year-old girl from Brooklyn, New York, *Dinky* was an immediate success. Between 1972 and 2009, thirty-six editions were published in five languages.

Gentlehands, a novel as successful as *Dinky* but without the humor, is a romance between a small-town boy and a rich, sophisticated Hamptons summer girl. The nickname of the boy's grandfather is Gentlehands, but he is anything but gentle. An escaped Holocaust concentration camp guard, he once took pleasure in torturing the female prisoners. His American family does not know about his past until the authorities track him down. Harrowing as the story is, the *New York Times* called it "important and useful as an introduction to the grotesque character of the Nazi period."

One of the hardest books for me to write was *Little Little*, my book about dwarfs. I kept worrying that I wouldn't get my little heroine's voice right. How would someone like that feel, a child so unlike others? After a while, I finally realized we had a lot in common. As a gay youngster, with no one I knew who was gay, I had no peers, no one like me to befriend—just like my teenage dwarf. She finally goes to a meeting of little people and finds friends, just as years later I finally met others like me in New York City.

I also used my experience being gay in a Kerr novel called *Deliver Us from Evie*. I set the story in Missouri, where I had studied journalism at the state university. I had been a tomboy, so I made my lead character, Evie, a butch lesbian. She is skillful at farm chores few females would be interested in, dresses boyishly, and has little interest in the one neighborhood boy who is attracted to her. I didn't want to feminize her to make her more acceptable, and I worried a bit that she would be too much for the critics. Fortunately, my readers liked Evie and her younger brother, Parr, who doesn't want to take over the family farm when he grows up. The book is now in two thousand libraries worldwide.

When I write for kids, I often draw on experiences I had when I was a teenager living in Auburn, New York—a prison city. All of us were fascinated by the large stone building in the center of town, with gun-carrying guards walking around its stone wall. Called Cayuga Prison (Auburn is in Cayuga County), it appears in several of my books. One of these books is called *Your Eyes in Stars*.

Growing up, I was friends with a boy whose family was in the funeral business. As the only male, he was expected to take over the business when he grew up. Can you imagine looking forward to that in your future? Neither could Jack, who inspired *I'll Love You When You're More Like Me*.

My book *Night Kites* is about AIDS. To my knowledge, it was the first print book that featured two gay men who have contracted AIDS, rather than having the illness come about because of a blood transfusion. When we first learned of AIDS in 1981, everyone grew afraid of old friends who were gay males. There was a cruel joke that "gay" stood for "got AIDS yet?" But soon we realized AIDS was not just a gay problem. The book is set in the Hamptons, though much of the action takes place on a Missouri farm.

I have also written a teenage autobiography, called *Me Me Me Me Me*, which deals with my years growing up in upstate New York during the thirties and forties. My older brother, Ellis, was a fighter pilot in the naval air force, seeing action over Japan. After World War II, he fought in Vietnam for our secret airline Air America, and later in Korea. He was my favorite relative until Vietnam. We had a major falling-out over the war when he called me a "peacenik." We never felt the same about each other after that, up until his death in the nineties. My much younger brother has lived with his family most of his life in Arizona. We don't see as much of each other as we'd like because of the distance between our homes.

I have always given my parents credit for my becoming a

writer. My father was a great reader. Our living room was filled with walls of books. I grew up with him reading to me, and ultimately began reading any novel he did. But I am a writer largely due to my mom's love of gossip. Our venetian blinds were always at a tilt in our house because Mother watched the neighbors day and night. Many of her telephone conversations began, "Wait till you hear this!" On execution nights in our prison, my mother and her girlfriends huddled outside in a car, waiting for the executioner to go inside. He was one of ten men who entered the prison together on execution night, so no one snooping could know who had really pulled the switch.

I have taught writing for thirty-four years at nearby Ashawagh Hall in East Hampton, where I've lived most of my adult life. We benefit, in part, the Springs Scholarship Fund. My teaching inspired me to write *Blood on the Forehead: What I Know about Writing*. A dozen members who had never finished a book became published writers after joining the class, and we also have members who are already professional writers. Currently, I am in the middle of a memoir called *Remind Me*. The title comes from an old Mabel Mercer song:

Remind me not to find you so attractive
Remind me that the world is full of men

EBOOKS BY M. E. KERR

FROM OPEN ROAD MEDIA

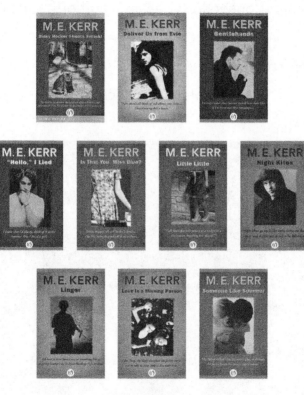

Available wherever ebooks are sold

OPEN ROAD
INTEGRATED MEDIA

OPEN ROAD

INTEGRATED MEDIA

Open Road Integrated Media is a digital publisher and multimedia content company. Open Road creates connections between authors and their audiences by marketing its ebooks through a new proprietary online platform, which uses premium video content and social media.

Videos, Archival Documents, and New Releases

Sign up for the Open Road Media newsletter and get news delivered straight to your inbox.

Sign up now at
www.openroadmedia.com/newsletters

FIND OUT MORE AT
WWW.OPENROADMEDIA.COM

FOLLOW US:
@openroadmedia and
Facebook.com/OpenRoadMedia

CPSIA information can be obtained at www.ICGtesting.com
Printed in the USA
BVOW08s1353280815

415326BV00001B/1/P